Five-Star Reader Reviews
for *Rendezvous with God*

These are several of the more than fifty five-star online reviews.

One of his best!

"Excellent read for anyone regardless of where they are on their spiritual journey. I can't wait for the next one!" —Carrie Maldonado

Another slam-dunk

"[W]hat sets this story apart from others and elevates it to the top of the heap is this: woven into a grand story is the unvarnished truth that we will all have one . . . a rendezvous with God . . . and we'd best be thinking about how that will play out." —Deb Gorman

A fresh take on a relationship with Jesus

"I really enjoyed Myers' wit and sense of humor that was peppered throughout the book. Readers who enjoy some humor and being provoked to think will like this book. I am curious to see how Myers continues the story in the next book, [*Temptation*]." —teachesgrade2

Fun, fast read

"Bill Myers has long been a favorite author, and this is a great addition to his works. Highly recommended as a quick beach/travel read." —klr3

Bill Myers hits it out of the park again

"I first discovered Bill Myers' writing when I stumbled across his book *Eli*. It became the book I thought everyone needed to read. I have gifted it many times over. I am back there again with *Rendezvous* — It has me thinking of Jesus and my relationship with him in a whole new and more personal way. Touching, emotional and thought provoking. I will be reading it again and recommending it to my friends and others— until the next one—which I hope I don't have to wait too long for." —Rochelle F.

Just like us, just like me

"WOW! Once again, Bill has written a book that we really need for right now. I know that Jesus is with me, but can you imagine carrying on a conversation and hearing Him as plain as day? Thank you, Bill Myers, for once again causing me to ask questions. But in a way that God/Jesus/The Holy Spirit would approve." —Susan K. Hand

This book is relatable! Hard to put down!!!!

"I HIGHLY RECOMMEND THIS BOOK! This is phenomenal! *Rendezvous with God* is not just your ordinary Fiction! It is written to bring you into the life of Jesus, as He walked the earth, His message, His life, but it also reveals a lot about ourselves and how we can communicate with the Lord and how we can have a REAL relationship with Jesus, and so much more! *Rendezvous with God* is RELATABLE! If you are looking to have closer fellowship with Jesus, this is the book for you. It's definitely for me." —Davina

Fun book from a favorite author

"For me, the book became increasingly powerful as the story line progressed—particularly at the climax of the novel. In addition to this core scene, I also found strong truths embedded throughout. One of my favorite emphases was the distinction between the 'Christian club' and the 'friend' of Yeshua . . ." —stephaniea11

Wonderful presentation of the gospel!

"What a powerful book! This compares to *Eli*, which is the first book I read by this author. While that book tackled the question of what would it look like if Jesus had come today instead of 2000 years ago. This one takes a person from the present and has him jump back in time to be taught directly by Jesus in Bible times. The lessons were poignant and the scenes were dramatic. It was such a unique and worthwhile way of presenting the gospel message. This is one I'd definitely recommend to any Christian and to anyone who is seeking to understand more about how a relationship with God works." —Erin L.

Get ready for an unexpected new perspective

"We know from the title that we'll be reading about encounters with God. But if you think that you are about to snooze through another bland, religious book, think again! Time and time again as I read, my responses were as surprised as those of the main character as he tumbled abruptly in and out of the present and the past. Several times my eyes flew wide open as things were said that shocked me—made me question the validity. But each time I realized that there was the ring of truth. The story is raw, pithy and full of pain, joy, humor and surprise. But I'm not telling you any more. Read it for yourself and see what happens to you!" —Gaye Lewis

Rendezvous with God

"Bill Myers' latest novel, *Rendezvous with God*, presents an intriguing question—what if you could talk to God face to face? In the novel, the main character, Will, finds himself transported in his dreams and then in visions to the time of Christ, where he interacts with Jesus one on one. The situations facing Jesus mirror the challenges in Will's own life, and Will grapples with faith as he navigates the unexpected arrival of his pregnant niece on his doorstep and his sister's drug overdose. Will's understanding of Christianity is challenged as Jesus shares the difference between having a relationship with Him and simply following rules. The book is an eye-opening experience with God in the midst of an interesting story. The discussion questions at the end of the book provide even more thought-provoking content, challenging readers to question their own perceptions of God and their faith. Great story with impact!" —WFM

A peek into a personal conversation with Jesus

"I loved it! I cried, laughed, and I even stopped breathing around chapter eighteen. *Rendezvous with God* is about a relationship, not about being in a club. The stick figures included help make the point. Other points are:
- It's about choices. Not A or B, but orange.
- It's about forgiveness. Not to excuse the past, but to free ourselves from it.

- It's about our focus on self-absorption and how we think too highly of ourselves. It's not about us, it's about Him, and the Him in us.

And while I read each page, one nagging thought lingered: this is powerful writing. This is how to use words to paint the value of brokenness and how God uses it. This is how good books are written." —Robin

Gripping story that is thought provoking and inspirational!

"I like everything Bill Myers has written but this book is different in that the main character directly speaks with Jesus at times in his present-day world and at other times slipping back into Jesus' world. But it is more than sermonizing. Our college professor hero has many serious real-life problems to deal with and Jesus helps him to find a way through the morass of very real human suffering. In addition to being a gripping story, the deeper meanings will give the reader plenty to think about. Highly recommend!" —M. Medberry

Wow. Simply: WOW!

"'The brightest victories hide in the darkest places' got an underline from me. I don't often underline works of fiction, but that line deserved it. Also, the line: 'God never plays defense.' —Wow. I also laughed out loud when Will pointed out Jarius, and Yeshua said, 'Now you're just showing off.' And the balloons at the end??? Way too perfect. Bon Voyage and hurry up and finish Book II. That's all I've got to say." —Eva Marie Everson

TEMPTATION

TEMPTATION

Rendezvous with God – Volume Two

Bill Myers

FIDELIS
PUBLISHING

*Discussion questions have been included
to facilitate personal and group study.*

Fidelis Publishing®
Sterling, VA • Nashville, TN
www.fidelispublishing.com

FIDELIS
PUBLISHING

ISBN: 9781956454024
ISBN: 9781956454031 (ebook)

Temptation (Rendezvous with God – Volume Two)

For information about special discounts for bulk purchases, please contact BulkBooks.com, call 1-888-959-5153 or email - cs@bulkbooks.com

Unless otherwise indicated, all Scripture comes from Holy Bible, New International Version®, NIV® Copyright ©1973, 1978, 1984, 2011 by Biblica, Inc.® Used by permission. All rights reserved worldwide.

(NASB) New American Standard Bible®, Copyright © 1960, 1971, 1977, 1995, 2020 by The Lockman Foundation. All rights reserved.

Published in association with Amaris Media International

Cover designed by Diana Lawrence
Interior design by LParnell Book Services

Manufactured in the United States of America

10 9 8 7 6 5 4 3 2 1

❦

Batter my heart, three-person'd God, for you
As yet but knock, breathe, shine, and seek to mend;
That I may rise and stand, o'erthrow me, and bend
Your force to break, blow, burn, and make me new.
I, like an usurp'd town to another due,
Labor to admit you, but oh, to no end;
Reason, your viceroy in me, me should defend,
But is captiv'd, and proves weak or untrue.
Yet dearly I love you, and would be lov'd fain,
But am betroth'd unto your enemy;
Divorce me, untie or break that knot again,
Take me to you, imprison me, for I,
Except you enthrall me, never shall be free,
Nor ever chaste, except you ravish me.

John Donne 1571–1631

❦

PART ONE

CHAPTER
ONE

"DR. THOMAS!" AN irritating voice cut through the din of students leaving with me from my British Lit class. "Dr. Thomas?"

I glanced over my shoulder to see Lucas Harrington, the all-school heartthrob, angling his way through the crowded hall toward me. Six foot two, articulate, and always late with assignments, at least those he bothered to complete. What he lacked in work ethics, he more than compensated in charm and manipulation. Think George Clooney meets Eddie Haskell.

He sidled up beside me and I asked, "What can I do for you, Lucas?"

"Great lecture today. Of course, they always are."

"Is this over your Charles Dickens's paper?"

"What? No. I promise I'll get that into you just as soon as my little brother finishes his chemo."

"I thought it was your sister."

"Her too."

"You have my sympathies."

"Thanks. Anyway, I just wanted to congratulate you on your big decision."

"Decision?"

"You know, to become a Christian."

I looked at him in surprise. "Who told you I'd—"

"Dr. Thomas." I turned and saw Gretchen Davis rolling up to my other side in her wheelchair. She was the real everything Lucas pretended to be. Thoughtful, sincere, and with so much joy, if you weren't careful, you could catch it. "Congratulations!" she chirped.

"For . . . ?"

"Jenny Buchanan said you received the Lord way back during the holidays."

"Christmas," Lucas corrected. "Not 'holidays,' Gretch. Christmas."

I glanced uneasily to the others around us. My choice was personal, not something for public consumption—at least not yet, and certainly not by my students. Not that I was trying to hide it. In a few weeks, when the time was right, I'd come out of the closet—though the weeks turned to months with Easter fast approaching.

The point is, I was careful to tell no one except Sean Fulton, a close friend of nearly ten years from the English department who, with John Lennon glasses and bow tie, was too busy being a free spirit to judge anyone. And, of course, Amber, my fourteen-year-old niece in the last stages of pregnancy who kept catching me with an open

Bible. Both were safe bets. Sean, because he promised confidentiality and I knew where all his bodies were buried (at least the dozen-plus who'd dumped him), and Amber, who didn't know anybody in my circle—well, except Darlene Pratford, a gregarious faculty member who never stopped talking and who—

I had my answer.

Gretchen reached out to give me a knuckle bump. "Welcome to the fam, Doc."

I returned it, lowering my voice. "Uh, thanks."

"So," Lucas continued, "me and Gretch, we were wondering if you'd like to be a sponsor."

"Sponsor?"

"For Bible Club," he said. "You know, the Christian club here on campus."

Gretchen added, "We meet over at Health Sciences every Thursday at noon."

"That's tomorrow," I said.

"That's right," she said.

"Don't you already have a sponsor?"

Lucas snorted. "Yeah, Dr. Swenson."

Gretchen came to Swenson's defense. "She's cool and everything, but it would be super to have two of you. You know, her and someone who's a bit more, uh . . ."

"Progressive," Lucas said. "The woman may be hot, but she can really be a tight—"

"Buttoned-down," Gretchen interrupted.

"Right," Lucas said, "buttoned-down."

We followed the crowd of students through the doors and into the afternoon sun. The morning's cold, gray mist—vintage weather for this time in Washington—lifted and it looked like we might actually be able to see a sunset. I veered to the side ramp for Gretchen's benefit (and for my back I threw out moving boxes of books last week).

"I appreciate the invite," I said, "but it's all pretty new to me. I've got lots to learn."

"Of course," Gretchen laughed. "No one knows everything about God."

"Except Doctor Swenson," Lucas smirked.

They traded grins which I pretended to ignore. Truth was, Dr. Patricia Swenson, over at the nursing school, was the most attractive woman on campus. Though a bit thin, she could easily pass for a model; the perfect Barbie prototype. The fact her husband Ken left her eighteen months ago was one of life's great mysteries. It also made her the target of any uninitiated faculty member (or overconfident student) who thought they could exploit the situation. It seldom took more than one encounter with that brilliant mind of hers to hamstring their egos. And, last semester, for that poor fool who tried to get physical with her . . . well, reports were her black belt in martial arts did appropriate damage to some appropriate areas.

"Seriously," Lucas continued, "you'd be perfect. I mean, all the students love you." I cut him a look. He countered,

"Well, most of them. Besides, Swenson is hot and you're both single."

"Lucas . . ." Gretchen admonished.

He shrugged. "I'm just saying. So, what do you think?"

"I think I'm not quite ready for something like that."

"No worries," Gretchen said. "But you're going to pray about it, right?"

"Right. I'll, uh," I threw another glance to the students around us, "I'll be sure to do that."

"Super," she said.

"Say, Dr. Thomas?"

"Yes, Lucas?"

"About that Dickens's paper?"

I took my cue and headed left on the gravel path leading to faculty parking. "I'll see you both in class tomorrow."

"And maybe noon at lunch?" Gretchen said.

"We'll see."

"Alright!" Lucas repeated. And, never able to leave well enough alone, he called out, "Praise the Lord! Right, Professor?"

Without turning back, I gave a half-wave—grateful to be exiting but feeling even more guilty for feeling grateful. What was wrong with me? After all I saw and heard, why couldn't I acknowledge becoming a—the word stuck in my throat like a chicken bone—Christian?

Not that I didn't have reasons. Weren't Christians the poster children for mindless bigots and intolerant hypocrites? Sure, there were exceptions—the J. R. R. Tolkiens and Mother Teresas of the world. But seriously, are they the first ones who come to mind when you mention the word? Particularly in this day? And don't even get me started on their politics. So how had I, a professor at a major university, next in line to chair my department—well, until that New Year's Eve fiasco at my house—taken such a reverse step in intelligence and now, social status?

Unfortunately, I knew the answer. Believe me, I knew. I also knew explaining how I was swept back in time for off-the-record chats with the man, himself, would do little to defend my position. I shook my head and climbed into the car, a faded green Honda Civic, circa 2010. Driving off campus, I took the I-5 and headed for Anacortes to catch the 4:42 ferry.

Of course, I had other concerns—not the least being my daily abandonment of Amber, all alone in the house with just the cat, the dog, and her schizophrenic adolescence. Actually, over the past few months, she'd been doing a lot better, and we were beginning to adjust to one another. In fact, we hardly ever fought—fighting would mean talking, and talking would involve looking up from her cell phone while simultaneously turning down Netflix. She also started taking GED classes over the internet and, at Darlene's insistence, was subjecting herself to prenatal checkups. We even managed to pass another child welfare visit—though it meant agreeing to convert my beloved office into her bedroom.

However, there were those incessant texts during class. Such dire emergencies as Karl, the cat has fleas, or why do we still have 2% milk in the fridge when she was clearly lactose intolerant? (For the record, we'd already gone vegan and were gluten-free.) Consequently, I made it my custom to avoid checking messages until I was on the freeway and heading home. Unfortunately, this afternoon, my phone, which had a battery life of roughly 2.3 minutes, was already dead. That left me with no alternative but to return to over-thinking my reaction to Lucas and Gretchen.

Cindy, my ex, always accused me of living in fear of what other people think. Maybe it's true. She certainly said it enough times. But it's not like I committed intellectual suicide by making the decision. I did my research. I won't bore you with what I discovered. Well, okay, I'm still a little defensive, so indulge me just a bit—like the hundreds of archeological sites confirming the Bible's accuracy—or the historians who can trace the life of Christ through ancient documents without once referring to the Bible—and how about those devout atheists who set out to disprove the resurrection then wound up becoming rabid believers?

Still, it was my encounters that did me in. Seriously, how could someone I saw to be so wise and caring con-stantly claim to be the only way to God? Not exactly a compassionate and open-minded scholar. Like C. S. Lewis, I couldn't wrap my mind around some "great teacher" making this and other outrageous claims. A raving egotist? Sure. A con artist? You bet. But not the loving, miracle worker I became so fond of.

So, was I a traitor for not running out and buying the latest "Jesus, My BFF" T-shirt or slapping some bumper sticker on my car? (For the record, "Nietzsche Is Dead: God" is my favorite.) I wasn't sure. But the guilt and questions dogged me all the way to the ferry terminal.

Once I boarded, parked the car, and headed out onto the deck to stretch my legs, it happened again. A hot wind hit me from behind. I turned and, just like old times, found myself transported to an arid, desolate countryside. I was part of a small crowd shouting and dragging him along the rim of a steep precipice.

CHAPTER
TWO

THERE WERE ABOUT a dozen of them; angry men encircling him, shoving him along the edge of a cliff. They held his arms, shouting to one another and screaming into his face, "Self-righteous bastard! Son of a whore! We know your brothers, your mother!"

I worked my way closer. As always, no one could see or hear me. Except for Yeshua. And, when our eyes finally connected, everything stopped. Not entirely, but everyone began moving in slow motion. Very slow motion. Their anger was still present, their mouths still opened in shouts and oaths, but their voices were barely audible—just faint, low rumblings. Except for Yeshua.

"Hey there," he said. "It's been a while." He didn't smile, but he was definitely not looking as concerned as he should be.

"Uh . . ." as usual I was at a loss for words, "impressive."

He leaned past a shouting face to better see me. "Time's a relative thing, remember?"

I nodded. It wasn't the first time I saw him defy the laws of physics. Nor was it the first time I saw him irritate people. I motioned to the surrounding mob. "Still not great at making friends, I see."

He broke into that smile of his. "Man's pride, God's truth—not always a good combo."

I pushed in closer, ducking under an upraised fist frozen in the air. "And this doesn't bother you? People hating you like this?"

He glanced around and sighed. "Not my first choice. But . . ."

"But what?" I asked.

"My identity is not wrapped up in what other people think of me."

I sensed a lesson coming and I wasn't wrong. "Are we talking about what happened back on campus?"

"You're still letting people determine your value. You keep seeing yourself through *their* lens."

"And the right lens is?"

"God's. The one seeing you as his loved son."

"Easy for you to say," I scoffed.

"Why is that?"

"You *are* his loved son."

"And so are you." I turned to him. Those golden-brown eyes were focused directly on me. "You have no idea how much Father and I adore you, do you?"

I glanced away, cleared my throat. "I think I saw that—up on the hill when you were being tortured to death."

"And who was that for, Will?"

I swallowed and looked to the ground. He waited. When I found my voice, it was clogged with emotion. "For me—you did it for me."

When he didn't respond, I looked up to see him staring off in the distance. Finally, he spoke, "And when I face that day, it will come from a passion so deep, you'll never fully understand."

"*When* you face it? You already went through it. I saw you." He looked back at me and I had the answer. "Right," I said, "time's a relative thing." I glanced at his hands. There were no scars, not like I saw the last time when he was fixing breakfast for his guys on the beach.

He continued, "What you saw on that hill was my love for you. One that values your life as greater than mine."

My vision blurred and I glanced away again.

"You have no idea how deeply we cherish you. And that, my friend, is your greatest weakness." I looked back to him as he continued, "If you grasped just a glimmer of our passion for you, the opinions of others, good or bad, would mean nothing." He motioned to the surrounding crowd. "Their words would be as indiscernible as they are now." He reached behind my ear and caught a rock that slowly floated toward my head.

I looked at it startled, then answered, "But their words, sometimes they're incredibly loud, overwhelming."

He nodded. "We'll always be with you, Will. Always."

I took a deep breath, knowing I should believe him.

He wasn't finished. "But remember, we're only part of the solution."

"Part?" I asked. "And the other is?"

"You."

I scowled, trying to understand. "I thought it was a free ride; things were supposed to get easier, now."

He broke out laughing and motioned to the crowd. "I'm sorry, does this look easier?"

"But that's why you came. You're supposed to do the heavy lifting, so we don't have to. For your glory, you said."

"No."

"No?"

"Paying for your sins is my glory. Your growth is what we accomplish together. Otherwise, you'd never learn to co-rule with me."

"Wait. What?"

"This next season is going to be tough. You're going to face huge problems. Temptations. But it's important you face them so my Spirit can grow within you, so you can rise above them."

"What about prayer?" I argued. "Isn't that supposed to make things easier? Prayer changes things, right?"

"Of course. And the greatest thing it changes is . . ." He waited for my full attention. "You. Not your circumstances. Circumstances come and go, but you, your soul, that's what will live forever. That's where our real interest lies."

I paused, thinking it through. "Which is why you don't always answer prayer?"

He shook his head. "We always answer prayer. Just in bigger ways than you expect. Sometimes we use situations to teach, so you'll develop and grow until you're bigger than the circumstance."

"*Teach, develop, grow.* You make it sound like I'm in some sort of training program."

"You are."

I gave him a look.

"But only if you want."

"And if I don't?"

He cocked his head at me, knowing I knew the answer.

"Free will," I said. "One of your favorite topics."

He nodded. "That's right. But people forget their freedom continues—all the way to the end."

"Meaning?"

"Too many of my followers quit, remaining infants who constantly soil their diapers." He looked away, sighing wearily. "Still, they're our children and we'll always love them." He focused back on me. "But for those who choose to continue—to become everything the Father and I dreamed they would be before we created them—then yes, you're in training and difficult circumstances are part of your development."

"To rule with you?" I said, making sure he heard my skepticism.

"And to judge angels."

I opened my mouth, but no words came.

"Now, if you'll excuse me." He reached out and placed the rock in the air where it had been, then moved me a step aside so it would miss my head. "I need to focus here. My old friends and neighbors want to show their appreciation for what I said by throwing me over this cliff."

Suddenly, I realized where we were—the angry men, the valley floor below. "Nazareth," I said. "This is your home town, where they tried to kill you?"

"Living out truth isn't always popular, but you have my word, if you keep saying yes and stay with the program, you, Will Thomas, will become whole and complete, lacking in absolutely nothing."

I could only stare.

"Oh, and remember"—there was no missing the twinkle in his eyes—"I never play defense."

And with that strange, foreboding encouragement, I was back on the ferry, standing on the deck, preparing for—well, I had no idea.

THREE

THE SUN HAD just set when I turned down the driveway. I was surprised to see the light spilling from the opened garage and out onto Darlene's parked BMW. Her visits never came this late. They were always early to midday since the last ferry departed the island at 9:18. If we were lucky, those visits sometimes included a killer Saturday or Sunday lunch. No complaint there.

Over the weeks, now months, since Amber lost her mother, the two became fast friends. And since they started putting their heads together to plan a baby shower, well, I'd never seen Amber so excited. To date, she made few if any acquaintances out here on the island, but Darlene, with her gregarious personality and over-abundance of friends, assured her the house would be packed with people . . . and gifts.

I was grateful for an older woman's influence—upon Amber, not myself. Don't get me wrong, Darleen was great—good sense of humor, easy on the eyes, but according to my friend Sean (a self-appointed expert on women), ever since my divorce, she had designs for me. It's not that I didn't enjoy her company, but my one time at-bat and strike-out with the opposite sex strongly suggested it was not my game. Whereas Darlene—well, her somewhat racy reputation indicated she didn't care how many innings she had to play to win.

Because of her investment of time and attention, I knew I'd eventually have to make it clear it was all about Amber and not about us. Last Sunday I realized it was now or never. Over a terrific spread of fried chicken, mashed potatoes and gravy, green beans with bacon, and biscuits, I broached the subject.

Her response wasn't exactly what I expected.

"What?" She looked at me, blinking in confusion. "What are you saying?"

"I just want to make sure you don't think that I'm . . . that you're . . . well, you know."

"No, Will, I don't know."

I cleared my throat and glanced to Amber who stared at me, then back to Darlene who also stared. "It's just, you coming over so often, I don't want you to misconstrue . . ." I cleared my throat again and reached for a glass of water.

"Misconstrue what?"

"It's just that . . ." I turned to Amber for help. She tilted her head with the same puzzled expression as Darlene. I tried again. "I just don't want to be giving you any false hope."

"Hope?"

"You know."

"What are you—" Suddenly, her eyes widened. "You think I have the hots for you?"

"What? No, of course not."

Amber snorted at the absurdity.

"Then what exactly are you saying?"

"I just . . ." I cleared my throat again. "I wanted to make sure that, you know—"

She forced a laugh. "Don't flatter yourself, Will Thomas."

My face grew warm. "I'm sorry. I didn't mean to—"

"Just because a person takes an interest in some sweet girl who recently lost her mother doesn't mean I have ulterior motives for—"

"No, of course not."

Amber snorted again. "Male egos."

They both shook their heads sharing scornful chuckles.

"I meant no disrespect," I said.

"Might have thought about that before you brought it up," Amber suggested. Chagrinned at my stupidity, I half-explained, half-apologized. "I just wanted to make sure there was no miscommunication."

"No," Darlene said, "you've communicated quite clearly."

"And I'm sorry, you know, for misinterpreting your, your . . ."

"Intentions?"

"Right. Your intentions."

I watched for some clue of what she was thinking. But she said nothing more—just a clear and very distinct, "Hmm," as she returned to her meal.

I looked to Amber who also resumed eating.

I wasn't sure what "hmm" meant, but recalling my past domestic blunders, I spent the rest of the meal trying to patch things up—complimenting her on the chicken, mentioning how the rain was letting up, and telling Amber how good she looked in the sweatshirt they just purchased—the one with all the factory-made tears—and how much did it cost again, not that it mattered? The point is I'd once again stepped in it. And, as usual, I wasn't exactly sure what the "it" was.

That had been less than a week ago, and things were finally returning to normal. But as I opened my car door, Darlene was already running from the garage.

"Will! Thank God! Where have you been?"

"I—"

"She called you a dozen times, but you never picked up!"

"My battery died," I said, climbing from the car. Is there a—"

"She's trapped."

"Amber's—"

"On one of those little islands out there with your dog."

"She took Siggy with her to—"

"I was down on the beach with your boat."

"You mean she didn't take my—"

"The tide was out. I looked for the motor but it's not there."

"It's being serviced, but I—"

"You've got oars somewhere, right?"

"Yes, they're in—"

"I've looked everywhere but—"

"The storage shed," I said, finally completing a sentence. As with Amber, my input in conversations was just a formality—a polite indulgence to allow my non-estrogened brain to catch up. "The storage shed," I repeated, motioning to the side of the garage. "They're in the storage shed."

She nodded and raced for it.

I followed. "Be careful, it can be—"

"Awfully muddy back here," she called.

"Right," I said. "So, tell me, exactly—"

"The tide was out and she went for a walk."

"On the flats? I told her never to walk out there by herself."

"She had Siggy."

"I told her—"

"You know kids."

But of course, I didn't. Another missing skill set. I joined Darlene at the shed and started going through my keys for the padlock. "So she—"

"Walked to one of those little islands, the tide came in and now she's stuck."

"Why didn't she—"

"She kept calling, but you never picked up."

"Right, my phone battery."

"I keep a charger in the car."

"Right, I should—"

"Probably wouldn't hurt to have one, with her being so pregnant and home alone."

I was unable to find the right key in the dark and asked, "Would you mind turning on your—"

Her cell phone light came on.

I found the correct key, unlocked the padlock, and after a little search-and-rescue, found the oars. While pulling them out, I managed to twist my already tweaked back. The pain was sharp. I thought I managed to hide it—until Darlene insisted on helping carry the oars to the beach.

As we headed down the slick, partially-decayed stairs, I asked, "Did she tell you which island?"

"The little one with fir trees."

That was a relief. Trees meant she wasn't marooned on one of the outcroppings of rock that disappear with every incoming tide. And fir trees nailed it down to a single choice: Hawk Island, a quarter-mile due west.

"You really should get a phone charger for your car," she said. "Remind me. I have an extra one."

We arrived at my ten-foot skiff, something out of a Rockwell painting, and pulled it across the sand into the water. Again, I was careful to keep the pain hidden, and yet, when we got into the water and pushed off, she insisted on rowing.

"What?" I said.

"Your back."

"There's nothing wrong with my—"

"Is that why you've been seeing a chiropractor?" (Seriously, was there nothing she and Amber didn't share?) She reached for the oars. "Here, let me."

"I'm fine," I said.

"Will, don't be a—"

"I said, I'm fine." Still having some old-school testosterone, I repeated, "I'm fine," and took a particularly deep stroke into the water to prove my point—while trying not to pass out from the pain.

"Hmm." was all she said.

The night was clearing and a moon, just shy of being full, peeked through the last of the clouds. We were 250 yards out when her cell rang—the love song from *Titanic*. She answered, "Hey, kiddo. We're almost there." She paused, then replied, "Really?" She turned toward the island, another 200 yards away. "Yes, yes, I see you!" Then to me, "Do you see her?"

Off to the left, on the island's beach, a pinpoint of light waved back and forth. Darlene raised her phone and waved it back as an answer—to which Amber turned hers off and on, to which Darlene turned hers off and on. And so it continued, the two communicating in yet another language I'd never understand—as I continued rowing, trying not to whimper, and pointing out to God now would be as good a time as any for one of my visits.

Apparently, he disagreed.

Minutes later, we slid onto the beach. Siggy raced at us, bounding and barking while a grateful and perturbed Amber approached—grateful to see Darlene, perturbed I'd not come sooner. At least Siggy was happy to see me. Nothing says I love you like a seventy-five-pound, wet and muddy golden retriever jumping all over you—though truth be told, it was probably just past his supper time.

FOUR

"THIS IS HARD," Amber whined as she pulled on the oars.

It was Darlene's idea to have Amber row a bit. "For a little exercise," she said—and, I suspect, to give my back a break.

"Uncle Will does it better."

"Equal rights are not special rights. Isn't that so, Will?"

I was clueless how to answer, particularly with Amber being so pregnant. But, over the weeks, I learned when it came to women's issues, it was always best to respond with a simple, knowing nod—though with all the "S" curves Amber was cutting in the water, it would probably take us an extra hour to get home.

"I think I'm getting a blister," she whined.

I gave another nod, an attempt to show just the right amount of compassion without getting sucked into an argument.

But Amber was a pro. "You know, if you'd let me drive none of this would happen."

"How's that?" I knew I'd regret asking, but curiosity exceeded common sense. Like I said, she's a pro.

"You know how whenever I get stressed, I get this need to go someplace, to clear my head. Kinda like a compulsion thing."

"No, I didn't know that."

"Right. Well, if you *ever* paid attention, you'd know."

It was another trap. This one I was smart enough to avoid.

"Anyways, so when I got that stupid D on that stupid online English essay, I had to take off and go somewhere. And since I don't have a license—"

"Or a car," I pointed out.

"We have Mom's."

"Which isn't safe to drive."

"And that's my fault?"

She had me there.

"So, since I don't have a license and I needed to go somewhere to blow off steam, here we are."

I thought of untangling her logic, but experience warned otherwise. Instead, I switched to my tried-and-true default: silence.

It wasn't long before the night's stillness settled over us. There was no sound—just the lap of water and the rhythmic creak and splash of Amber's oars. Moonlight reflected off the gentle swells while, beside and behind us, phosphorescent, blue-green plankton glittered, glowing like a thousand fireflies.

Darlene sighed. "Isn't this wonderful?" She took a deep breath. "The smell of water, the salt, all these colors; everything wrapped in such peace and quiet." I watched as she snuggled deeper into her coat and closed her eyes. She was right, of course. This is why Cindy and I moved out here—away from the city, nearly an hour from work—because of the silence, the beauty, that indefinable connection to something greater, something all around us. But that was so long ago. Over the years of work, the rut of routines, and a disintegrating marriage, the place became, well, just a place. Almost a nuisance with its upkeep, and drizzle, and subject to ferry schedules.

But now, experiencing it with Darlene, through her eyes, I felt it again. As it used to be. She took another breath and sighed, looking into the night sky filled with stars, shaking back her rich, auburn-red hair. I was struck by the way moonlight played off her face and, yes, how it bathed a figure more ample than some in their twenties, but still engaging.

Suddenly she sat up. "Look at that."

I turned and followed her gaze to the north. A luminescent sheet of green glimmered in the sky.

"Is that—" Darlene turned to me in wonder. "Are those the Northern Lights?"

I nodded. We watched as they slowly rippled like a giant curtain above the trees. In all the years I'd been on the island this was only the second time I saw them.

"Amazing," she whispered.

I looked on in equal awe. But it was more than the lights. Or the stillness. Or the ocean. There was something else—embers stirring deep inside me, feelings I thought long dead.

She turned to Amber, "Do you see it, kiddo? Is that cool or what?"

"I gotta pee," Amber said.

I shook my head and came to my senses when the boat suddenly lunged and water sprayed over us. I thought it was some sort of rogue wave until I heard the roaring wind and shouting men. I wiped the water from my eyes and saw I was at the back of a much larger boat from a much different time. I'd been here a few months earlier when we encountered the crazy man with the demons. As before, I sat on the bench where Yeshua lay stretched out and asleep. Up front, his men shouted and screamed as the boat shook and heaved. I gripped the bench so I wouldn't be thrown to the floor.

Yeshua opened his eyes, took a moment to focus and spotted me. "Will?"

The bow dropped into a wave. Water swept into the boat as the men continued to yell.

"You're sleeping through this?" I shouted.

He shrugged. "Long day."

"Am I . . . is this that big storm on Galilee?" I yelled.

"The likes of which they've never seen."

I looked back to the men as they began to scramble and bail water.

He continued, "Remember about being on top of circumstances instead of under them?" The ship's bow rose steeply. It was a strange time for a lecture. Then, again, no stranger than the last.

"By connecting with you?" I yelled.

"*Abiding,* that's right." We crested the wave and began to fall. I braced myself as he calmly continued. "Faith is a muscle. If you don't use it, it atrophies."

We slammed into the water.

"This is some workout!" I shouted.

He nodded, stuffing his blanket and cushions into a dry corner. "Great champions need great workouts. And these guys are Olympians."

"Wake the master!" someone screamed. "We're all going to die!"

He smiled. "Eventually."

Another wave crashed into the boat causing it to shudder violently.

"So, all of this, it's for them?" I shouted.

"And you."

"I *had* my workout! Last January, remember?"

"One trip to the gym doesn't make an athlete."

"Who said anything about—" The boat dipped and swung hard to the left. We braced ourselves as water rushed in, swirling around our feet. "I read your Bible!"

He gave me a look.

"Isn't that enough?"

"Rule books explain the game."

"Exactly."

"They're no substitute for playing."

"Playing?" I shouted. "Playing what? What game?"

"*My* word becoming *your* flesh. Moving from your head to your heart."

Another wave, the biggest yet, slammed into the boat, causing an ominous groan and loud *CRACK*.

Seeing my fear, he said, "Relax—it gets easier in time." We caught another swell, a huge mountain of water, carrying us even higher. "My presence just demands practice."

"This is crazy!"

He laughed. "By world standards." The boat crested then tilted down. "But my peace is greater than the world." We shot down the wave, men crying, screaming as the bow plunged under water, disappearing a moment before surfacing.

"Could sure use some of that peace now!" I yelled.

"Then abide."

"How?"

"Worship."

"*Now?* That's crazy!"

"Didn't we just cover that?"

I looked down at the water, now up to my calves, as Yeshua grabbed the blanket and cushions in the dry corner. "I've got a little shut-eye to catch." To my astonishment, he stretched back onto the bench and snuggly wedged himself in.

"You're kidding me!"

"You've read. We've talked." He slipped a cushion under his head. "Now practice."

"Practice?"

He pulled up the blanket. "Am I greater than the storm?"

"Yes, of course . . . I think."

He closed his eyes. "Then enjoy."

"You just can't—"

"Tomorrow's a busy day." He turned and readjusted his blanket. Discussion over.

But not the storm. The boat shuddered so violently I thought it would break apart. We continued taking on water as the men continued to yell and bail. I read how storms suddenly appear on Galilee with winds reaching near-hurricane force. We were there now.

The bow shot into the air again, impossibly steep. We crested and I braced myself as we tilted, almost vertically, and began to fall, men screaming all the way until we crashed, water pouring in.

"We're swamped! Wake the master!"

I looked to Yeshua. Unbelievable. He was either asleep or doing a pretty good job of faking it.

Peter, the big man I remembered from before, sloshed through the water toward us. Drenched, barely able to keep his balance, he shouted, "Lord!" Another wall of water hit; the force so great it knocked him to his knees. Unable to stand, he crawled to us. "Teacher!" He reached up and shook Yeshua. "Teacher, don't you care we're perishing?"

Yeshua turned to face him.

"Save us, Lord!"

"Why are you afraid?" he asked.

Peter stared at the absurdity of the question.

Yeshua sat up and shook his head, softly mumbling, "So little faith." He pushed aside the blanket, threw his feet over the bench, and waded forward through the water. Peter and I followed behind. Up front, the men clung to the sides of the boat, the ropes, the mast—anything they could find as the bow lifted high into the air. As we crested, Yeshua raised his hand and shouted. A single word. But spoken with absolute authority. "Stop!"

Instantly, the wind ceased. *Instantly*. We stared. But he wasn't through. Directing his attention to the sea, he spoke again, this time more quietly, "Hush. Be still."

The wave immediately flattened, allowing the boat to settle gently back into the water.

Silence was absolute. There was no sound except dripping water from the mast and ropes, and the gentle sloshing around our feet. No one spoke. What could be said? They looked to each other, the sea, the sky.

Yeshua turned back to face them. For the first time I can remember, I saw disappointment in his eyes. Yet mixed with a certain compassion. And pity. "Why?" he asked.

No one dared answer. None looked him in the eye.

"Why do you still not have faith?"

CHAPTER
FIVE

SIX HOURS LATER, I lay on the sofa in my living room, unable to sleep—my thoughts a jumble of crashing waves, shouting men—and Darlene's moonlit face tilted up in wonder at the night sky. Also included were fragments of our dinner conversation after the little excursion to the island. During her visits, Darlene never stooped to cooking something as mundane as macaroni and cheese. But with no time to shop and limited to our overflowing larder of gluten-free, lactose-free, taste-free, macaroni and cheese (Amber has a thing for macaroni and cheese)—it served as our dinner—along with an impressive cucumber salad Darlene "threw together" to supplement our green-deprived existence.

After the usual chatter about the baby shower and how we better hurry and have it before the baby is born, our talk turned to overnight accommodations.

"No problem," Amber said after polishing off her second glass of chocolate soy milk. "Darlene can sleep in your bed."

I shot her a look. "I don't know what you think you're proposing, young lady, but—"

"And you sleep on the sofa," Amber finished.

I blinked, "And I sleep . . ."

"What do you think I meant?" she asked.

Both women turned to me.

I cleared my throat. "Right. No. That's a good idea." I felt my ears growing hot.

Amber belched.

"I wouldn't want to impose," Darlene said. "Surely there's a motel on the island."

"We're lucky to have a Safeway and hardware store," Amber said. "But, hey, if you want, I can sleep on the sofa."

"Not in your condition," I said.

"What's that supposed to mean?"

"I'm just saying—"

Darlene came to my rescue. "He means it's probably hard enough for you to find a comfortable position in a regular bed let alone the sofa."

"You got that right," Amber said.

"No." I cleared my throat again. "You're right. I'll sleep on the sofa, it'll be fine."

"Are you sure?" Darlene asked.

"No problem."

And it was true, sleeping on the sofa would not be a problem. The problem would come the next day when our colleagues at school learned Darlene spent the night.

Not that they'd have to know, but with Darlene's abundant communication skills and the department's eagerness for gossip, the odds were not in my favor.

"C'mon then," Amber said as she struggled to rise from the table. "I'll help you change the sheets." I glanced at Darlene, surprised to hear Amber offer help to anybody with anything.

"What about the dishes?" Darlene asked as she rose.

"I've got them," I said and started gathering the plates.

"You sure?"

I nodded.

Amber was halfway out of the room when she spun back to us. "What about pajamas?" Just as quickly, she had an answer. "I bet Aunt Cindy left something behind." Then to Darlene, "Unless you like sleeping in the nude?"

Darlene grinned as she joined her. "Depends."

They both giggled as they started for the hallway.

"Actually," I coughed slightly, "I don't know if that's such a good—"

"No, of course not, your uncle is right," Darlene said.

"About the pajamas," Amber asked, "or . . ."

"I think he meant the pajamas." Then back to me, Darlene teased, "That is what you meant, right, Will?" I fumbled for an answer. Sensing my embarrassment, she eased up, but just a touch. "Maybe you have something else I could wear? Like one of your old shirts or something?"

"Shirt?"

"You know something nice and cozy I can slip into."

"Um—"

"Don't worry," Amber said, taking her hand. "We'll find something." They started down the hall. "What about a toothbrush?"

"In my car," Darlene answered.

"You carry a toothbrush?"

"It's the twenty-first century. A girl can't be too prepared." More giggles as they disappeared.

It was that last comment that stuck in my head—or at least kept me staring up at the living room ceiling as I lay on the sofa. An alluring woman in my bed, all alone, in one of my shirts—or not. What did Sean say back at the Christmas party? *She wants you, dude. Have you been out of circulation so long you don't recognize the signals?* And that look of wonder on her face out in the boat in the moonlight. All stirring up feelings I'd long forgotten. Or thought I had.

No. I pushed the thoughts from my mind. I was too old for that sort of thing, much less with the likes of Darlene Pratford. Don't get me wrong, she was smart, big-hearted, definitely spirited—and for reasons that made no sense, interested in me (unless, as Amber pointed out, my male ego was working overtime). The point is, she definitely lived in the fast lane while I, well, I didn't even know where the onramp was.

I forced myself to think of other things. The conversation with Lucas and Gretchen. My embarrassment at being outed as a Christian. Their asking if I'd join Patricia Swenson in sponsoring their Bible Club. Patricia Swenson. Brilliant, drop-dead gorgeous. Maybe it wouldn't hurt to swing by her classroom just to say hi. I mean, here was someone well-educated and deeply devoted to God. And if her group really did need my help, maybe we could discuss it over coffee, start to get to know one another, and—

Stop it! What was happening to me? I rolled onto my side and stared at the back of the sofa. A relationship was the last thing I needed and, to be honest, probably even capable of. Seriously, what was I thinking?

I closed my eyes and immediately felt a familiar hot breeze against my face. I sat up to see I was sitting beside him on a small stone wall. Low, rolling hills surrounded us; a dozen shades of brown and a heat so dry you could smell it. Not far away, a dirt path led to a short, circular stack of stones. A well as far as I could tell.

"You're back," he said.

I nodded, glancing around. The place was completely deserted. "Where are the guys?"

"In town. I sent them to get supplies."

"*All* of them?"

He smiled. "A lesson on loving their enemies. Every one of them despises the people living in this area. Long story, but lots of hate and bigotry. I didn't want any of them to miss out on the training."

"More *training*," I said.

"Only for those I love. So, what about you, what's happening?"

"Not much."

"Which is why you stopped by."

"I thought these meetings were *your* doing?"

He suppressed a smile and repeated, "So how are you?"

I shrugged. He waited, knowing I'd come around. I took a breath then waded in. "I just have a question."

"Only one?"

"Or two."

"Good."

"Maybe," I said. He cocked his head, waiting and I continued. "It's about sex." Quickly, I added, "Listen, I understand if it's not appropriate to—"

"'Appropriate?'"

"With you being God and all."

He broke out laughing. "What? I can create it, but I can't talk about it?"

"Right, right. But, I mean—were you ever tempted?"

"With sex?"

I immediately backtracked. "I'm sorry, that's way too irreverent, I didn't mean—"

"Excuse me?" he interrupted. "A thirty-year-old, healthy male, totally celibate, and you don't think I'm tempted?"

"You're God."

"Incarnate. In the *flesh*. I have to face every temptation you face and then some."

"But with God's power so you're not—"

"*Flesh*, Will. Same problems, same limitations." He motioned around us. "Otherwise, this would all be a cheat. I could never relate to your struggles and sorrows—or your temptations."

"So . . . you really can be tempted?"

"Was I tempted in the wilderness when you were with me?"

"Well, yes, but—"

"The boys are gone. I'm about to meet a woman so promiscuous other women in the village won't even associate with her, who's had five husbands and is now living with someone who isn't even—"

"Samaria?" I interrupted. I motioned to the well. "You're about to meet the woman at the well in Samaria?"

He nodded. "Where my people never visit, so no one would ever know. Just the woman and me, all alone."

"And you'll overcome the temptation through sheer obedience."

"Yes . . . and no."

I frowned.

"It's the Father's love in me—and his love for her—that gives me the power to obey."

"His love overrides your temptation?"

"Yes. But not just here. The same goes for every temptation to sin." He paused, letting the thought take hold. When I had the slightest grasp, he continued. "I never teach sin management, Will. That's religion at its worst. You don't try not to sin. You simply abide more deeply in our presence."

"And that removes temptation?"

"No. You'll always have temptation. It's a matter of letting us replace it with something better."

"Your love."

"And our presence, yes. It always comes down to relationship. If you abide in us, and allow us to abide in you, our presence will push back any temptation."

"Like the balloon metaphor from our earlier times."

He nodded. "Your body. Our Breath."

I took another moment to chew on it.

"But you have another question."

I shook my head. "No, not really."

"Will . . ." His tone made it clear he knew there was more.

Reluctantly, I continued. "But, in my day and age . . ." I hesitated.

"Go on."

"I mean, with birth control and everything, is sex outside of marriage really that wrong?"

"Sex *is* marriage." He saw my surprise and explained. "We designed it to be the outward experience of a more intimate, spiritual encounter."

"*Spiritual*—" He lost me. "What?"

"Think Plato's cave. The shadow on the wall is nothing compared to what's casting it. Trying to experience the physical without the spiritual is as empty as seeking satisfaction from the shadow instead of its reality."

"But . . . if both parties are willing and nobody gets hurt—"

"*Everybody* gets hurt. That's why it's sin. You think we arbitrarily decide what is sin and what isn't? It's all about your protection. Every word we speak is for you—whether you understand why or not."

"But—I don't mean to be argumentative, but how does it hurt?"

"Your body and spirit are intimately connected. There's nothing your body does that doesn't impact your spirit. And vice versa."

"But," I countered, "it's just sex. Even animals do it."

"Stop!" His outburst shocked me. "You are more than animals! You are eternal, spiritual creatures. Created in our image."

I'd never seen him quite so worked up and I wasn't sure how to respond.

He took a moment to gather his composure, then continued. "Yes, if you want, you can go at it like animals. But as higher creatures, whose bodies and spirits are united, sexual intercourse without spiritual intercourse belittles and demeans your soul."

"But," I proceeded cautiously, "people have casual sex all the time."

"Each time degrading their spirit. You treat women, the bearers of your children, as a superfluous means to momentary pleasure."

"Women want casual sex as much as men." He appeared startled. I tried not to smile. "It's called *equality*."

"And you find humor in that?"

"I . . ."

"To your shame, you've exploited the nurturing tenderness we gave to woman. You've forced her to build callouses around her heart so she can be like you."

"Not me, personally. I just—"

"She was to raise man to her level, not be dragged down to his."

He looked away. I watched as he took a moment to touch his eyes. This time I had the good sense to remain silent. When he resumed speaking, his voice was soft, but thicker. "You can't imagine the anguish of watching our children debase themselves into nothing more than rutting animals."

I wasn't sure what I could say, even if I wanted to. Moments passed until, off in the distance, I spotted a figure approaching on the path, its image wavering in the heat.

"Is that her?" I asked.

He turned and shaded his eyes. "Yes. Inside, her soul is parched and withering—desperate to quench a thirst the wells of men can never satisfy." He gathered his robe and stood.

I rose with him. "And she'll listen to you?"

"She'll duck and weave to try and change the subject, but she'll eventually come around."

"Okay if I stay and listen?"

He shook his head. "For the temptation to be complete, it's best we be alone." He started toward the well to meet her. "But I'm sure you'll be able to read about it."

I nodded then called out. "Say, listen, I'm sorry about this."

He turned to me. "About what?"

"Seems I'm always bothering you with my mess."

His eyes gave that familiar sparkle followed by a grin. "If I was afraid of mess, Will, I would never have created you."

I grinned back, then realized it may not have exactly been a compliment.

Before I could respond, I heard running water. I blinked and discovered I'd returned to staring at the back of the sofa. Behind me, in the kitchen, someone was at the sink. I turned to see moonlight flooding the room through the picture windows. The faucet shut off. A moment later, glass in hand, Darlene padded past me in bare feet, wearing one of my dress shirts.

I spoke quietly so not to startle her. "Hey there. Everything okay?"

She slowed to a stop in front of the windows, her outline softly diffused in my shirt by the moonlight. "Oh," she said. "I didn't mean to disturb you."

"No, I was still awake."

"Funny, me too." She shook back her hair. "I guess neither one of us can sleep."

I swallowed, unsure how to respond.

She saved me the effort. Glancing down the hall, she added, "That's one big bed. Don't know about you, but I could sure stand for a little company."

As inviting as it was—the hair, the shirt, the silhouette—and, trust me, it was inviting—I felt a wave of sadness. Pity. Because at that moment all I saw was a lost and lonely little girl.

I found my voice and answered, "Thanks, but I'm good."

"You sure?"

"Yeah. I'm sure."

"Alright, then." She turned and started down the hall.

"Darlene?"

She slowed.

There was so much I wanted to say—she didn't have to be alone, there was someone who adored her, who would satisfy her deeper thirst. Instead, I took the coward's way out and simply said, "Good night."

She responded in kind and headed down the hall into the darkness.

CHAPTER
SIX

EARLY THE NEXT morning we were on the ferry heading to the mainland—Darlene and I in our separate cars. Well, I was in my car. Darlene was topside having coffee and chatting away with whoever would listen. She definitely had a gift.

And me? I was checking my online Bible for what I might have missed about the woman at the well. He was right, of course. Not only about her past but in the way she tried to dodge the real issue—attempting to turn the tables to prevent him from getting too close: *"Who do you think you are? Are you a prophet? You're worshiping at the wrong place."* An interesting defense. One I suppose we all resort to. Certainly, the one Darlene had used earlier at breakfast.

After cheery greetings, small talk about our upcoming classes, and Darlene's insistence upon fixing us toast, fried eggs, and some bacon she found stuffed in the back of the freezer (Amber wouldn't be up until noon), I knew I should broach the obvious.

"Listen," I said, "about last night."

"Forget it," she said. "I was totally out of line." She started to rise. "You want some juice? I see you have some orange juice in the—"

"No. Thanks. I'm fine." As she sat back down, I continued. "It's just, well, I've been going through a lot of changes."

"So I hear." I looked at her and she continued. "Amber said you've gotten religion. I should have been more sensitive."

"I don't know if 'religion' is the right—"

"I just figured, you know, we're not children." She reached for her coffee mug. "And if two consenting adults with perfectly healthy needs . . ." She let the phrase hang as she took a sip. "But if you feel you have to, I don't know, repress them for some higher whatever, well—I really should have been more sensitive."

"I'm not sure 'repress' is the right word."

"Repress, deny, whatever."

I let it go and continued. "It's just—well, I think I've found something better."

She arched an eyebrow. "Better than sex?"

I smiled. "Well, at least that type of sex." The words barely escaped before I wondered if I stepped in it again.

"Meaning?" I hesitated and she confirmed my suspicions. "No, don't tell me," she reached for the toast and some jam. "A roll in the hay with some promiscuous, middle-aged—"

"No, no, that's not it."

"Hmm." She focused on spreading the jam.

"I think you're a terrific person," I said. "Charming, articulate . . ."

"Some say a bit too gifted in that area."

"Smart, attractive. And the way you're connecting with Amber, it's like you're some kind of, I don't know, *teen whisperer*."

"Yeah. Too bad I'm going to hell, right?"

"I never said—"

"Listen, Will." She looked up from the toast. "I don't want to be offensive. You're a sweet guy. It's just I had a taste of what you're talking about a long time ago."

"You did?"

"Let's just say it didn't work out."

I looked at her, waiting for more.

"I had an uncle, elder in our church, who was—well, let's say he didn't practice what he preached." She bit into the toast and began chewing.

"I'm sorry to hear that."

"Water under the bridge."

But I could tell it wasn't. I tried again. "The thing is, what I'm reading about him, about Jesus, well, he's pretty impressive."

"A great teacher," she said, continuing to chew. "I'll give you that."

"He made some crazy promises. And so far, at least for me, he's delivered." I hesitated, then continued. "And if he's delivered for me, I'm betting he can do that for anyone."

"Including some schlumpy, biology professor hungry for sex?"

I glanced at my eggs, this time having the good sense not to answer—which, once again, was the wrong answer.

"I appreciate what you're saying, Will, I really do. But it's not for me. Besides, my life is pretty full. I doubt I'd have time to squeeze in all that church-going, not to mention picketing abortion clinics, attending anti-LGBTQ rallies and voting Republican." She laughed. "Voting Republican—not exactly sure that'd keep me out of hell."

I smiled at the joke and backed off, letting her lead us into other topics—something we were both grateful for. Soon we were discussing politics, the school and, yes, even the weather. The point is, I met my responsibility. I did the right thing and owned up to what I believed. But if it was the right thing, how come it felt so wrong?

Back in my car on the ferry, I chewed on the thoughts until I was interrupted by my phone. I glanced at the number but didn't recognize it. Nothing unusual, not even with being on the national *Don't Call* list. Against my better judgment, I picked up.

"Hello."

"Will?" It was Sean, my friend from the English department. His voice was hoarse and strained. "Thank God you picked up."

"You sound terrible."

"You have Belinda's number?"

Belinda was a mutual lawyer friend I'd known since grad school.

"Sure," I said, "what's going—"

"You've got to call her for me."

"Alright. Why can't you?"

"I'm in jail."

"You're what?"

"Bellingham courthouse."

"What happened?"

"One of my students—she filed a complaint."

"A complaint? For what?"

He hesitated, then answered. "Sexual assault."

CHAPTER

SEVEN

THEY SAY MEN my age are lucky to have one close friend. I'm not sure why. Maybe we start dying off. Maybe we're more solitary. Or maybe we get so involved with our families (or our wives' families) we just don't take the time. Whatever the reason, I count it a privilege to call Sean Fulton my friend. Probably my best. Not that I'd ever admit it, particularly to him. We don't send each other cards or gifts—which would entail knowing each other's birthdays—and we can go days, weeks without talking.

But we've always been there for each other—he was the best man at my wedding and sounding board over the weeks, day or night, when it failed—me during his DUI days and ongoing fight to stay sober. Because of our differences, some call us Mutt and Jeff. He loves crowds and being the center of attention. I am content to remain in solitude. And yet, despite being such polar opposites, if there ever was an example of a friend closer than a brother, it was Sean.

That's why his call was a shock. Yes, he considered himself God's gift to women, and yes, he had enough stories to make any adolescent boy drool (and some of us middle-agers). But he was no fool. He knew where the line was. And as the women's movement grew more and more restrictive (his word, not mine), he behaved himself accordingly. The man's moral compass didn't always point true north, but at least he had one. I don't know what he did or didn't do, but I know Sean Fulton. And I know he wasn't stupid enough or immoral enough to get involved with one of his students.

Belinda, our lawyer friend, knew that too. She assured me over the phone she'd have him out of jail by noon and there was no reason for me to cancel classes to visit him. She also assured me that if charges were not dropped, his biggest battle wouldn't be in the halls of justice but in the court of public opinion.

If the first day was an example, she couldn't have been more right.

Word spread across campus like wildfire. Whoever the accuser was, she'd told a trusted friend, no doubt in the strictest confidence, which meant the entire campus knew by noon. There were plenty of rumors of who the victim might be, but little doubt over the assailant and his guilt. And since we were colleagues in the same department and many knew of our friendship, I became his reluctant defense attorney.

"Hey, Dr. Thomas, you hear what happened?"

"Hey, Dr. Thomas, you think he did it?"

"Hey, Dr. Thomas, any idea who he did it to?"

I had no problem remaining loyal. Yet, at the same time, I knew there were plenty of women, no doubt even on campus, who bore the lifelong scars of sexual assault from other men (my sister and mother having been living proof). It was a tricky balance. I didn't want to discount their experiences or discourage future victims from speaking out against their assailants, but as I said, I knew Sean.

For this and probably a half dozen other reasons, I decided to take Lucas and Gretchen up on the invitation to attend their Bible Club over at Health Sciences. It wasn't a large group, just twenty or so students sitting at desks eating lunch. Dr. Patricia Swenson sat with perfect posture on the front desk eating thinly sliced apples, cheese, and rye crackers. She wore a green and white tartan scarf, nicely-tailored beige blouse, and a forest-green skirt. I did my best to ignore the sculptured legs stretching the rest of the way to the floor.

Over the years we spoke a few times and this was no different—I, struggling to overcome my usual social clumsiness and she, responding with a polite smile. Moments later, Gretchen rolled forward in her chair to open the group in prayer. Then, after covering old business about the upcoming Easter break and the Walk for Life fundraiser, she introduced me. And the debate began. Not about Sean, but about how God regards women in general.

"Is the Bible as misogynistic as some claim?"

"Why were Jesus's twelve disciples all men?"

"Was Paul's instruction to women directed at a specific church with a specific problem or to all women?"

I was impressed at their passion, not to mention intimidated by how well they knew the Bible. In my high school youth group days—well, the three or four meetings I attended—our purpose was mostly to check out the girls. With this group it seemed entirely different. Not that sex didn't enter the discussion—after all, we are talking about kids in their late teens and early twenties—but it took at least ten minutes to get us there.

Meanwhile, my thoughts had already returned to Sean. Belinda said she'd have him out by noon. It was 12:25. I decided to give him a call and started to slip out of the room when Patricia called over to me, "And what's your opinion, Dr. Thomas?"

I turned back. "I'm sorry, what?"

"On sex?"

"Oh," I said. "Huge fan."

The kids laughed. I guessed they were surprised it's still a hot topic for people over forty—well, all right, closer to fifty. But, seeing I had their attention, I continued (after all, I am a teacher, making any opportunity to lecture difficult to decline). "God is too," I said. "In fact, did you know in Jesus's day, when a couple was about to have sex for the first time, the entire village would gather outside their house and eagerly wait for the news?"

There were the expected snickers and more than a few *eewes*. A quick glance to Patricia indicated she was not exactly thrilled with my overshare but, as you may remember, I was eye-witness to just such an event. "That's right," I said. "And when they finished, the entire village broke into cheers and would celebrate for a week. That's how important they considered sex."

Patricia quickly stepped in, "*After* they were married."

I caught her look and added just as quickly, "Yes, yes, after they were married. Marriage first. Absolutely."

"But if you plan to get married?" a co-ed in baggy sweats and Army coat asked.

"Right," another kid added. "I mean, living together is okay. A trial, to see if you're right for each other."

"Exactly," Baggy Sweats agreed, along with a handful of others.

"Actually, from my experience—" I was about to share the last download I received from Yeshua at the well, but Patricia cut me off. Not that I blamed her. Particularly given my last response.

"According to studies from the University of Michigan, the opposite is true," she said. "Their findings indicate marriages which begin with co-habitation have a divorce rate of 86 percent."

"Seriously?" some platinum-haired kid asked.

"Yes, seriously. That's 36 percent higher than the national average."

"Why?" Baggy Sweats asked.

"I believe it's because those who cohabitate view marriage as something strictly for themselves—*What's in it for me? How does he satisfy me? How does she validate me?* But when their good times hit difficulties, as do all relationships, they choose the easy way out—instead of working through those difficulties and growing more deeply into one another."

"So, if marriage isn't about feeling good," some guy in a Seahawk's stocking hat asked, "What's it about?"

"Sex," someone called out.

Over a spattering of chuckles, Patricia asked, "And what do you do the other twenty-three hours?"

Lucas chimed in. "Or in Ian's case, twenty-three hours and fifty-four minutes."

More chuckles.

Patricia gave a tight smile. "Marriage is about a lot of things, including having children and raising a family. But one thing it's not about, and that's *you*." The class settled, and she continued. "It's about your partner. How you can make *them* happy, how you can fulfill *them*."

This was obviously news to the group. And, in part, a reminder to me.

"Check out Luke 6:38." She waited as they pulled out their Bible apps. Once they found the verse, she recited it by memory: "*Give, and it will be given to you. A good measure, pressed down, shaken together and running over, will be poured into your lap. For with the measure you use, it will be measured to you.*"

She paused, letting it sink in before continuing. "That's Jesus Christ talking. I'm not certain how that works. It makes no logical sense, and yet some way the more of my life I pour into others, particularly my spouse, the more life I should receive. Not immediately, perhaps, but eventually."

As I watched and listened to Patricia, my admiration grew. This woman was more than pretty gift wrapping. Or a Bible thumper. There was a depth to her, a substance. And the business about marriage partners living for each other. Isn't that what I always believed? What I tried to practice with Cindy—before she ran off with her boy toy?

Patricia continued. "The vows made in marriage, the type of marriage God has in mind, are to be permanent— as permanent as God's vows to us. Which means, even on my worst days at my worst behavior, I know he won't leave me. Nor I him. That bond, that trust, that's the very core of marriage."

Yes, I thought. *Yes!* All this time I imagined I was the only one who thought like this. I was the only one who believed in some fantasy world of ever-lasting romance.

But no, there was somebody else. And the more she spoke, the more my admiration grew.

"What about love?" Gretchen asked.

"Love's important," Patricia agreed, "but commitment is equally important. Feelings of love come and go. But a love based on commitment lasts forever."

Platinum Hair spoke up. "But casual sex is okay. I mean in dating and stuff."

"Yeah, dating's different," another agreed.

Patricia hesitated, the look on her face questioning if anything she'd said stuck.

"Dr. Thomas?" Lucas called to me from across the room. "You've been dating Dr. Pratford for a few months now."

"I've been what?"

"I mean, she's always going out to your place, right?"

I blinked. "We're, just uh, we're just good friends."

The class chuckled as if they knew better.

"So, when she sleeps over at your place, you guys just what, hang out and play Monopoly?"

"Lucas," Patricia scolded. "Dr. Thomas is our guest. His personal life is not your business, nor mine. But to address the previous question, premarital sex carries lots of baggage. There's no sense of exclusivity. There's always the comparison factor, along with the fear of giving yourself entirely to a temporary partner. Then there's the issue of becoming pregnant, not to mention STDs." The class was already growing bored, but she forged ahead. "For sexually active students, ages fifteen to twenty-five, the rate of STD is 50 percent. That's one out of two."

"Thank God for condoms," someone called out.

Without missing a beat, she countered, "Whose failure rate can be up to 14 percent. That's one out of seven."

I'll spare you the rest of the sex education class. Let's just say Patricia Swenson knew her stuff. And what she'd said about love and marriage, well, that's all I ever wanted with Cindy—two people, together, forever—"for richer or poorer, in sickness and health, for better or worse." We said those vows. But as soon as the shine wore off, so did her commitment—and my belief that such a relationship was even possible.

Now, after I threw in the towel, when I was certain only dead poets and myself believed such things, along comes this breathtaking beauty who not only believes it but is unafraid to teach it. Granted, as Lucas said, she may be wired a bit too tight, but her words, the conviction behind them, resonated so deeply and thoroughly inside me, I knew I had to talk with her further.

I waited until the last of the students left the room, then sucked up the courage and approached. "Patricia?"

She looked up from packing her book satchel. "So, what did you think?" she asked.

"Not your typical Sunday school class."

She smiled.

"Listen, I uh." I coughed and tried again. "I may have given the wrong impression."

"About?"

"You know, the whole premarital sex thing."

"How you choose to live your life is your decision."

"Right, but . . ."

She hesitated a moment, then chose to speak her mind. "But as a teacher, you should know—what does James say? 'Not many of you should become teachers . . . because you know that we who teach will be judged more strictly.'"

"I'll take your word on that."

"The children look up to us, Doctor. Like it or not, we serve as their role models on Christian behavior. That said—" She paused. I nodded for her to continue. "Are you certain Bible Club is right for you?"

I shook my head. "No. No, I'm not certain at all. It's all so new to me and I have so much to learn."

She nodded as she slipped on her coat.

"But what you said about marriage, about relationships? I couldn't agree more."

"I'm a '*huge fan*,' of truth," she said.

I grimaced at my earlier sex gaffe. "I know," I said. "And I thought you handled that perfectly. Throughout the entire class, the way you articulated truth, your choice of words, it was, well, superb."

"That's high praise from an English professor." She heaved the book bag onto her shoulder and prepared to leave.

My opportunity was slipping away. If I made my move, it had better be now.

"I know I have a lot to learn and that's why I thought—" I took a breath and went for broke. "Maybe you could show me a bit more of the ropes. Help me understand what's in that great big book you seem to know so well."

She didn't answer, seeming to think it over as we headed for the door.

Encouraged, I pressed on. "You know, maybe over a cup of coffee? Or dinner? Maybe I could take you out someplace and we could continue our discussion—or discussions." I winced, wondering if that last bit was too much.

She didn't seem phased. "You know," she said, "I jog every morning, on the mountain trail next to campus. Maybe you could join me on a run sometime."

"Sure." My voice cracked like some adolescent—despite my loathing of exercise or anything to do with sweat. "And then, maybe we could catch a breakfast after that." If I was going down, I was going down in flames.

She smiled—it may have been forced, I couldn't tell. "I appreciate the offer," she said as we stepped into the hallway. "But perhaps it would be better for you to find a men's group to study with."

"Sure. I mean, that's a great idea too. But—"

Something caught her attention and she added, "Besides, I'd hate for Dr. Pratford to misinterpret our actions."

"Darlene?" I asked.

She answered with a nod down the hall. I followed her gaze to see Darlene approaching. What on earth was she doing on this side of campus?

"Hi guys," she chirped. "Patty. You're looking hot, as always."

Patricia gave another one of those smiles. "Darlene."

"We were just talking about you," I said.

"Something juicy, I hope."

"I was explaining how, despite the rumors, there's nothing going on between us."

"Us? You and me?" Darlene scoffed. "Please."

"Exactly," I said. "We're just friends."

"If that."

Unsure how to respond, I continued, "Anyway, Darlene here, she's been taking a great interest in my niece who is living with me."

"You know, the pregnant fourteen-year-old," Darlene said. "The one that old slugger, here, wound up in the hospital fighting over at his New Year's party?"

Patricia nodded. "Ah, yes."

"Speaking of which." Darlene reached into her purse and pulled out a four-by-four, white envelope. "I just got these invitations printed up. For her baby shower." She handed it to Patricia. "It's Sunday. We'd love for you to come."

"Thank you, but—I don't even know the young lady."

"Exactly. The kid's got no friends and when it comes to role models, well she could stand for at least one positive one—right, Will?"

I cleared my throat. "You'd certainly be welcome."

"Which reminds me." Darlene reopened her purse. "I've got that phone charger we discussed." She pulled out a white cable and handed it to me. "Should help us stay in better touch."

"Thanks."

"Well, gotta fly." She turned, then, remembering something else, she turned back to me. "Oh, I think I left my earrings on your nightstand. The nice diamond ones? Be a dear and keep them safe, okay?"

"Uh—" I cleared my throat again. "Sure."

She looked back into her purse and resumed digging. For what I hadn't a clue.

Patricia glanced at her watch. "Listen," she said, "I really should be going."

"Of course," Darlene said.

"Right," I agreed.

"It was nice seeing you again, Darlene."

"You too, Patty," she said, continuing to dig in her purse.

Patricia gave me a polite nod. "Will."

I returned it, stepping aside to let her pass. I watched as she continued down the hall, pushed open the door, and disappeared. Only then did Darlene look up and see my crestfallen expression.

"I'm sorry," she said, "did I interrupt something?"

CHAPTER
EIGHT

THE FIRST WISPS of fog were moving in on campus as I climbed into my car. I'd barely left the parking area before Belinda called and hit me with some unwelcomed news.

"What do you mean it's complicated?" I said. "You promised he'd be out by noon?"

"Under normal circumstances, yes."

"Normal circumstances?"

"It may take an extra day or two, but don't you worry, we'll get him out and put this whole mess behind him."

"I don't understand. Who's pressing charges?"

"Proprietary information. At least for now."

"Proprietary?" I shook my head. "It doesn't matter. I'm going to head over and visit him."

"Visiting hours are over."

"Then I'll cancel class and see him tomorrow."

"I'm not sure that's such a good idea."

I blew out my breath in frustration. "And why is that?"

"I doubt your administration would approve."

"Approve? I don't need their approval." She didn't respond. "Belinda?" Still nothing. "Bel?" My mind raced. "You don't think he's guilty?"

"No, absolutely not."

"Then why—"

"If this goes viral, we'll all need to proceed with caution."

"Caution?"

"The college will want to distance themselves. Having you involved could only complicate matters."

"Viral? Distance themselves? What's going on? Bel, who's the accuser? Belinda?"

After a moment, she answered. "Benjamin Smock."

"The old rock and roller?"

"Who's just released an album and is trying to make a comeback."

"That's absurd. Sean's totally straight."

"It's not Smock."

"Then who?"

"Juliane DiGamo. His granddaughter."

෨

All afternoon and into the evening Belinda's information sat like a boulder on my chest. She'd been adamant that I do nothing. Any involvement on my part, no matter how slight, risked drawing attention—something she felt could hinder Sean's release. So, I was expected to just sit tight while my best friend spent another night in jail, his reputation shredded. She assured me things would be different tomorrow morning or early afternoon. Until then, I was expected to go home, have dinner, and relax.

I managed two out of three.

It was 8:30 when I finally retired to my office—laundry room with card table since Amber moved in.

"Karl, get down." Once again I pushed the cat away from my computer and off the table, and once again he was back up. Why he was attracted to me was anybody's guess. As Cindy's cat, I figured it should be just the opposite—like owner, like pet. But wherever I turned, he was under foot. Or, in this case, on keyboard. "Karl!" I pushed him aside and continued staring at the screen. If I couldn't deal with Sean and his issue, it was time to at least deal with the other. The one finally coming to a head during Amber's latest decree.

I should have been on my guard when I saw she had fixed dinner. Not that she didn't occasionally cook. For Amber, it was a little like playing house and, when edible, it was a win/win for both of us. But it was the steak she fried that threw me. Not the fact it was charred beyond recognition on the outside and just slightly warmer than a popsicle inside—patience in cooking (along with everything else) was not her strong suit—but the fact it was actually meat, since purging the house of all animal products had been one of her first missions.

"So . . ." I said, trying not to grimace after swallowing the first bite, "where did you find this? The back of the freezer?"

"They delivered it."

"They?"

"Yeah, I was walking to the store when Darlene called."

"Store? You mean Safeway? That's an eight-mile walk from here."

"Which I wouldn't have to do if I knew how to drive. Anyways, Darlene called and said to go home and she'd have them deliver."

"Darlene had this delivered?"

"She gets the dangers of a woman in my condition—doing all that walking, all alone, all by myself, which I wouldn't have to do if—"

"—I taught you how to drive."

"Exactly. But she said not to worry 'cause when she comes out Saturday, she'll give me a lesson."

"Darlene said she's going to give you a driving lesson?"

"Of course."

"Even though she's aware I said no?"

"What aren't you getting? Why do you think I'm being all nice and fixing you a steak and everything—though the smell was enough to make me puke."

"Figuratively."

"I'm pregnant, remember?"

I glanced at the meat.

"Don't worry, I washed it off." She continued, "Did she tell you about the baby shower?"

"I heard about it today," I said.

"But you knew we were planning it."

"Right. I just didn't expect it to be here."

"I told her you wouldn't mind. You don't mind, do you?"

"I—"

"It won't be a lot of people. Whoever she can dig up." Before I could answer, she continued. "You think she's too pushy, don't you? She said you'd think that, but I told her you're not always such a stuffy-butt."

"Stuffy—?"

"That deep inside you really appreciate her help. And her companionship."

"You told her—"

"She liked that. Especially the companionship part."

I gave her a look.

"You can thank me later."

"Listen," I said. "I appreciate the gesture. But lately, I mean, doesn't she seem to be a bit too . . . —involved in our lives?"

"What's wrong with that?"

"Well, nothing. Unless . . ."

"At least she's in touch with her feelings. She understands the sensitive side of being a woman."

"No argument there," I said. "But you have to admit, I am trying. Right?"

"Is that why you won't let me drive?"

"I don't think driving while you're underage is necessarily a woman's issue."

"You see. That's exactly what I'm talking about." Her voice grew higher. "Every time I try to share my deepest, heartfelt feelings, you shoot me down."

"Driving is not a deep, heartfelt—"

"And now you're telling me how to feel."

"I'm not—"

"Bang, bang, bang! Just shoot me down."

"I'm not—Amber, listen, I don't—"

"That's just it!" She grew shriller. "You *never* listen!"

"I—"

"At least Darlene does. And she cares."

"I care. And Darlene's not the issue here."

"Says who? You?"

"I—"

"Bang, bang, bang!"

"Amber."

She pushed herself up from the table. "There's just no reasoning with you when you're like this."

"Reasoning with *me*?"

She turned for the hallway. "You're such a chauvinist."

"Chauvinist? What is this, the '90s? Do you even know what that means?"

"Wow, now I'm being mansplained."

"Mansplained?"

"Look it up." She waddled down the hall toward her room.

"Amber, don't walk away. Ambrosia?"

She cocked her thumbs, pointing her index fingers at the ceiling, "Bang, bang, bang!"

"Amber."

She threw open her door and disappeared, slamming it.

That had been 45 minutes ago. Now, after clearing the table and sending Siggy into canine heaven with some frozen-fried steak, I sat in the laundry room staring at the screen. I wasn't surprised by Amber's zig-zag reasoning. Over the months, my negotiating her slalom course of logic had become a staple. But every once in a while, some truth emerged. And tonight, in fact for the past several days, that truth seemed to focus on Darlene Pratford.

Were her motives as altruistic as she claimed? Not that I blamed her, given Amber's miscues. But it seemed everywhere I turned, Darlene was there: my school, my home, my family (for what it was), and my social life (for what it wasn't). Please understand, the last thing I wanted to do was hurt Darlene's feelings and yet, maybe it was time to establish a few boundaries. Yes, I tried a little of this before, with no success. But this time I'd be clearer in presenting my concerns so she could fully understand.

I pushed Karl aside—well enough to reach most of the keyboard—and began typing a kind but firm email.

Hey, Darlene:

First of all, I can't thank you enough for all the ways you've stepped in and helped with Amber. Seriously, in these past few months, you've made such a difference in her life. But I'm wondering. Maybe it's time we should start . . .

I paused, looking for the right phrase. Sitting back, I took a sip of cold coffee and stared at the screen. There was no sound—only the faint stirring of grass from the night breeze. Grass? Night breeze? I turned and saw I was sitting on a grassy knoll above a familiar-looking lake.

NINE

I SEARCHED THE hill and spotted him not far away, perched on a rock overlooking the dark, placid waters. He saw me and we traded nods. I headed to him and as I arrived he scooted over to make room.

"You're alone," I said. "Again."

He nodded. "As often as possible."

"For someone who loves people, you sure spend a lot of time by yourself."

Glancing at the mug of coffee in my hand, he said, "For somebody who hates its taste, you sure drink enough of that."

"It's the drugs."

He smiled. "In 1,500 years my followers are going to try and outlaw it."

"You're kidding?"

"'The drink of the devil,' they'll call it."

"Doesn't look like it stuck."

"Never come between a man and his coffee."

"Amen." I took a sip. "Seriously though, for loving people, you sure spend a lot of time away from them."

"It's *because* I love them."

"Come again?"

"In silence, in solitude, this is where I best hear our Father's voice."

I nodded, thinking. "Not much chance of that in my world. Finding silence, I mean."

"A bit noisy where you come from?"

"And busy. Non-stop morning to night. If he does talk, I doubt I'd ever hear him."

Yeshua sighed quietly. "The cares of the world. They're like weeds. If you don't keep them pulled, they grow until they choke out what's really important."

"And that is . . . ?"

He turned to me. "Friendship. Yours and mine."

I glanced down at my mug, a bit ashamed we didn't spend more time together. Knowing he knew my thoughts, I replied, "I'm sorry—it's just, there's always so much going on."

He nodded and looked back over the lake. "His first line of attack."

"Attack? Whose?"

"Your adversary, the devil. He wants to steal from you—and, if possible, to kill and destroy."

I felt myself tense a bit. "Seriously?"

"Cutting you off from God's voice, that's his first step."

I frowned. "What exactly does it sound like? His voice, I mean? I know I heard it when we were up on that mountain with Peter and a couple of the guys—when Moses and Elijah showed up."

"When you caught a glimpse of my glory?"

I nodded. "And it must be great, you being so special you can hear him whenever you want, but for me—"

"No."

"No?"

"Hearing him because I'm special would be another cheat. Remember, I'm living with the same limitations as you."

"But you do hear him, right?"

"All the time."

"So, what's it like?"

He paused, thinking a moment before he answered. "God's voice is seldom audible. What you heard on the mountain was an exception. Usually, his voice is very quiet. A soft, barely distinguishable—*knowing*."

I motioned to the hill around us. "And people hear him best in places like this?"

"In solitude, yes. By leaving behind your day-to-day clamor and drawing down, deep inside yourself."

"Inside *myself*?" I asked in surprise.

"Where else would we talk with you? Burning bushes are a rarity."

"Okay, but—"

"What do you suppose happened when you asked us to come *inside* and be your Lord?"

"That's not a metaphor?"

"Your body is your temple, Will. Where we commune and break bread with you. And when you enter that temple, by becoming still and abiding in our presence, you hear us."

"That sounds a little Buddhist, New Agey to me."

"I'm not talking about emptying your mind. I'm talking about filling it. With our presence."

"But—how? I mean, that's easy to say, but how exactly do I do it? Am I just supposed to sit around like some lump and wait for something to happen?"

He smiled softly. "No. You encourage your soul to quietly savor us. Gently. In silent murmurs of wonder and adoration. Deep calling unto deep. And as the eternal swells inside you, our union becomes so intimate, there are times you won't know where your voice ends, and ours begins."

I quietly quoted, "'*Be still and know I'm God.*'"

He nodded. "From the Psalms. David had a crazy life, but he knew how to abide. And have you read about Elijah yet?"

"Um, it's a pretty big book."

He looked back out over the lake. "A few centuries ago, Elijah had a giant scare from a world leader. So intimidating, he ran off to a mountain to hide and, well, to pout a little."

"I thought he was a big-time prophet?"

"Even prophets have off days. Anyway, we told him to wait on a mountain for us; we were going to stop by for a visit. He did. And there's this great wind, so powerful it shakes loose boulders from the mountain. But he doesn't hear a thing from us. Not a word. Then he's hit with an earthquake. Huge. Still nothing. Then a major fire."

"A little dramatic, wouldn't you say?"

"Sometimes special effects are necessary to get your attention. But he still doesn't hear us. Not in the storm, not in the earthquake, not in the fire. And then, we finally speak—but in the softest, gentlest whispers."

I sat a moment, absorbing the implication. "So, I hear God when I get really quiet, listening to his presence inside me."

"That's one way, yes. Though there are others."

"Others?"

"Like studying the Scriptures we've spoken into."

"A bit daunting, though. Like I said, it's a pretty big book."

He smiled. "Which is why the Holy Spirit highlights it for you."

"Highlights?"

"When you're reading and suddenly a verse leaps off the page and grabs you."

"That's the Holy Spirit?"

"One of his jobs, yes."

"Must be a busy fellow."

"He likes it that way. And he doesn't stop there. Because if you listen carefully enough, you can hear us everywhere: in art, music, nature—even in your daily, mundane chores. And just as importantly, you can hear us by being still and listening to others—friends, strangers, even enemies." He turned back to me. "But you have to listen carefully—not simply waiting for them to stop talking so you can start. You have to listen deeply—past the words on their lips to the meaning in their heart. Because I'll tell you something, Will. The greatest love comes from those who listen the most deeply."

"Listening equals love?"

"When you silence your own noisy ego, you'll hear truth. Not the situation or people's words, but real truth—just as surely as I can hear you."

"I thought you were just kind of like, you know, a mind reader."

He smiled. "I'm a heart reader, Will. Of yours . . . and the Father's."

I took a deep breath, trying to understand how this all fit with my current dilemma. "So, the letter I'm trying to write, what should I say?"

"Letter?" Something in his voice indicated he wasn't particularly fond of the word.

"You don't like letters?" I asked.

"Sometimes they're the best example of *not* listening."

"How so?"

"They become one-way conversations. Instead of deeply communicating, you can wind up talking without listening." He shook his head. "Some of the greatest misunderstandings, and wounded relationships, even wars have started that way."

"But I've tried talking to her face to face."

"Instead of talking to her face to face, try *listening* to her heart to heart. Practice the humble act of listening. Deeply."

I scowled back into my coffee. When I looked up, it was into the glow of my computer screen. I glanced at the clock above the washer/dryer—9:52. If I called Darlene now, I wouldn't be off the phone until after midnight. But there was tomorrow. Tomorrow I would talk . . . and listen.

I would also do everything I could to help Sean.

And before all that, if I caught the first ferry in the morning, I might arrive at the campus just early enough to do a little jogging.

CHAPTER

TEN

"YOU OKAY?" PATRICIA stopped running long enough to look back at me. I was bent over, trying not to pass out.

"Yeah," I gasped, "just . . . something . . . in my . . . throat." *Like both of my lungs.*

She trotted back and joined me, motioning to a bench along the path. "Maybe you should sit down."

"It's just been . . . a little . . . while . . ."

She took my arm and guided me to the bench. "Since you've run?" she asked.

I nodded, thinking the last time was probably back in my high school track days. Why people subject themselves to this type of punishment is beyond me.

"You're looking a little pale," she said, easing me onto the bench. "Drop your head between your knees."

I did, which was a good way to stay conscious as well as coughing up a little of the morning's breakfast. I swore then looked up, apologizing on both accounts. "Sorry."

Ignoring me, she reached for my wrist to take my pulse. "You sure you're okay?"

"Yeah . . . I . . ."

"Shh," she said, "just breathe."

It seemed a good idea.

So far, the morning had been great. I caught the earliest ferry and, with the help of Siri, found the beginning of the running trail; a course heavily wooded with firs and cedars just east of campus. Then it was a mere fifty-five-minute wait until she showed up. Of course, she was surprised to see me and maybe, I hoped, a little impressed. In any case, after some vigorous stretching (involving a pulled muscle or two), and a silent note to self about picking up some Advil before class, we started our run.

By the first hundred yards it was clear she would be the one responsible for any talking. Not because I was practicing Yeshua's suggestion of deep listening, but because it was the surest way to avoid oxygen deprivation. It took several minutes for her to let down her guard, but once she realized how harmless I was, she began opening up. She shared how she was raised in the jungles of Papa New Guinea by missionary parents—a strict, austere childhood which she was now grateful for as it prepared her to face the temptations of today's "evil and adulterous generation."

Not that it made her superior, she explained. She had plenty of weaknesses—like her compulsion for order and neatness, her feelings of never quite fitting in. And, of course, guilt—to this day she still feels a twinge of remorse when only using a teabag once.

Eventually the topic rolled around to our faith and her church.

"And where do you go?" she asked.

"Well . . ." I wheezed.

"Fellowship is important."

"Absolutely."

"*Not forsaking the assembling of ourselves together*," she quoted.

I nodded. "Still shopping," I said, then coughed, hoping she wouldn't quote something about "*bearing false witness*."

"You're certainly welcome to visit mine," she said.

"Really?"

"Of course, it's not one of those liberal, feel-good places."

"Of course."

"Where all they do is preach cheap grace."

"Cheap grace?"

"You know, love this, love that, but nothing about holiness."

"Right."

"And we sing real hymns, not those mindless 7-11 ones."

"7-11?"

"Seven words repeated eleven times. Which, as you may know, studies indicate are no different than heathen chanting—a way to work oneself into an altered, emotional state."

"I thought it was so us old-timers could remember the words."

She laughed. Maybe it was forced. I couldn't tell. Either way, it made my heart swell. Alright, maybe it was my ego; as a guy, it can be hard to tell the difference.

"Our parson, Dr. Stewart, was a theoretical physicist. Very intellectual, very bright. I think you'd like him."

I nodded, trying to breathe—while appearing to be a sensitive listener. Not that I was intentionally misusing Yeshua's instruction, but obedience does have its rewards.

Back on the bench, my pulse slowed to something a little less life-threatening and Patricia rose to her feet, anxious to continue.

"Listen," I said, "why don't you go on without me."

"No, I can wait."

"Seriously, I'll be fine."

She glanced down the trail, then to her Smartwatch. "It's just—I really try to keep my heart rate above 100."

"Go, go," I said. "I've got a class coming up anyway."

"Are you certain?"

"Absolutely."

"Well, alright, then. I certainly enjoyed our time together."

"Me too," I said.

"Well, okay then. You're certain?"

I nodded.

She nodded back then turned and started down the path into the morning sun—as graceful and beautiful as any gazelle. Sensing my gaze, she looked back over her shoulder.

"See you at church!" I called.

She gave a thumbs-up, then turned and rounded the bend out of sight.

I took a few more deep breaths and rose for the slow but victorious walk back to my car. I had seized the day and I had won—or at least not come off a total idiot. Sean would be proud.

As I approached the car, my phone rang. I pulled it from my pocket and read the ID. It was Belinda, his lawyer.

PART TWO

ELEVEN

"WELL," BELINDA SPOKE through the phone, "I worked my magic."

"He's out?"

"They're processing him now."

"Great." I reached for my keys and unlocked the car. "I'm on my way."

"Will—"

I cut her off. "I know, I know, the school."

"It's going to be a massive PR problem. They'll do their best to distance themselves from him, and well they should. And so should you."

"He's my friend."

"And mine. But their reputation is on the block here. And you're a faculty member, a *tenured* faculty member."

"You're serious?"

"For the good of the school, yes I am. He'll understand. We'll hire Uber to get him home."

"Bel—"

"Look. Talk on the phone. 24/7 for all I care. But no texts or emails. And definitely no personal contact. Not until all this blows over."

I hesitated.

"Will?"

I remained silent.

"He'll understand. Listen, I've got court this morning; otherwise, I'd drive him home, myself. But as your attorney, as your friend, as a friend to both of you, please, *no* personal contact."

"I hear you."

"I know you hear me, but—"

"Let me think about it, okay?"

"Think hard. This is serious stuff. Particularly in today's climate."

"I get it."

"I'm not sure you do."

I rubbed my forehead, saying nothing.

"Okay. I'm gone. I'll check in later. But, Will—"

"Right, right," I said. "We'll talk later."

After hanging up, I slumped behind the wheel and sat there thinking. Western Washington University is a terrific school. I love it. So does Sean, as does the rest of the faculty. We'd all worked hard to raise the bar and be taken as seriously as the U of W or Washington State. A scandal like this, regardless how unfounded, could seriously damage our reputation, something neither Sean nor I wanted. But he was my friend. As with me, any family he had was either dead or moved to parts unknown. If I didn't stand beside him, who would?

I fired up the car and the seat belt alarm chimed. "Dear God," I whispered, "what should I do?"

No answer. But it didn't stop me.

"Go? Don't go? Just tell me."

Nothing but the alarm.

"C'mon. You say you answer prayer. This isn't even for me. Just give me a sign, some direction."

The chiming continued.

"Why won't you help? I'm trying to do what you want. Just show me. Yes? No? Go? Stay? Come on."

Nothing.

I dropped the car into gear, muttering, "And you wonder why folks don't pray. Why bother asking if you don't bother answering." I pulled from the parking lot and shaded my eyes with my hand to avoid the bright morning sun. When I withdrew it, I was sitting beside Yeshua on white, limestone steps, part of a much larger structure where dozens of people were milling.

"Hey, Will."

I toyed with not answering, figuring I'd return the favor.

"You're not sulking, are you?" When I still didn't answer, he rose. "Come with me."

I hesitated, then got to my feet and followed. We entered the structure along with a handful of his men. The place was a large courtyard filled with people. Many had their hands raised in prayer, others sat in small groups talking. I moved to Yeshua's side but he remained silent. If it was a waiting game, despite my best efforts, I lost.

"So, what about Sean?" I finally asked.

"Your friend."

"It's a simple question, should I pick him up or not?"

"What do you think?"

"If I knew, I wouldn't be asking."

We continued to walk.

"You say pray," I said. "So I pray. But you're not answering."

"I always answer."

I tried not to scoff.

"You just don't see it, that's all. There are too many moving parts; some you'll never be aware of."

"He's a friend," I said. "A good friend who needs my support."

"Then support him."

"If I do, I'll jeopardize something equally as important."

He nodded.

"So, what do I do?"

"What do you want to do?"

"I don't know!" I checked my frustration and brought it down a notch. "That's why I'm asking you."

"Maybe you're asking the wrong question."

"It's a simple question. Do I support him or not? Yes or no?"

Before he could answer, Peter called over the crowd. "Teacher?" We turned to see the big man pointing at a ragged beggar sitting on the ground—the beggar's face was crimson, burnt from the sun, some places black and peeling. His eyes oozed a milky pus drying to crusty brown patches on his cheeks. "Who sinned to make this guy born blind?" Peter asked. "Him or his parents?"

Yeshua turned to me. "Give me a moment." I nodded and he crossed over to the man and kneeled beside him.

Peter hovered over them and repeated, "Which is it, Lord?"

Yeshua looked intensely at the beggar and answered, "It's not this man's sin."

"Then his parents," Peter said.

"No. It's neither this man's sins nor his parents'."

"But—" Peter looked puzzled. "It has to be one or the other."

Yeshua shook his head. "This happened so the works of God can be displayed in him." As he spoke, he scooped up a small amount of dirt and spit into it. "As long as it's day, I'm here to do the work of him who sent me." With his thumb, he worked the spit into the dirt making a small glob of mud. "Because night is coming, when no one can work."

He reached to the beggar's face. Feeling his touch, the man flinched. Yeshua leaned over and whispered something which calmed him, but only slightly. Then, scooping the mud onto his fingertips, Yeshua gently dabbed it onto the man's closed eyes. A crowd was gathering and we all watched in silence as he continued to speak, "While I am in the world, I am the light of the world."

At last he finished. Rising, he helped the man to his feet. "Now, go," he said. "Wash in the Pool of Siloam." He nodded for Peter to help the man whose eyes were still covered in mud. Peter took his arm, gently turned him and guided him through the crowded courtyard. Yeshua watched a moment before turning to rejoin me.

"I read about that," I said.

He nodded.

"But spit?"

"A superstition," he said. "People believe the spit of a holy man has healing powers."

"Does it?"

"Of course not."

"Then why . . . ?"

"I meet people where they are." He shot me a grin, making it clear he was also speaking about me. "And if it takes something as harmless as spit to prime the pump of their faith, I see no problem."

We resumed walking. "Now, where were we?" he said. "Oh, yes, you'd asked a question and I answered it."

"No, you didn't. That's the whole point of this . . ." I slowed to a stop then looked back to where the blind man had been. "Was that—was *that* my answer?"

He smiled. "We've covered this before, Will. My answers are always bigger than your questions." I nodded, remembering bits of past conversations. He continued, "By limiting my response, you're limiting my power. And my love."

I quietly repeated the question I just heard. "'Which is it, Lord—his sins or his parents?'"

"And my answer?"

"Neither."

"Because?"

"You were answering something bigger."

He grinned, clasping my shoulder. "See. You *are* getting it."

"But—how does that answer *my* question?"

"It doesn't. Not on the surface. Sometimes my 'no's' just mean 'dig deeper.'"

"Into the situation?"

"Sometimes. Or, more often, deeper into me."

"So . . . when I'm struggling with a question and I don't hear your answer—"

"I'm calling you deeper."

"But how does that help me in the now, in the situations of the moment?"

"It's never just the situation, Will. Everything you encounter, in any area, is also about . . ." He waited for my answer.

"You?" I said.

He nodded. "And you. Our friendship."

"You're always saying that."

"Then start practicing it."

"I don't—"

"Go deeper, discover how the situation can be used for your growth and our relationship. Circumstances come and go. But you and me, we're eternal."

I scowled.

"Don't look to my hands to fix things, Will. Look into my eyes to know me."

And suddenly I was back in the car with the seat belt alarm chiming. I'd still received no clear-cut answer. Then again, maybe I had. Instead of coming to him as some cosmic Ouija Board for a *YES/NO,* I was to look into him for a deeper answer. I reached for my seat belt and buckled in.

The alarm stopped as I turned north to head for the courthouse.

TWELVE

I'D BARELY HIT the road before my phone rang. I pulled it from my pocket and saw Sean's number. "Hey," I answered, "just talked to Belinda. She says you're out."

"Free at last, free at last, thank God almighty, I'm free at last."

"If that's your Martin Luther King, it needs work."

"So, you coming, or what?"

"I'll be there in ten. Sounds like we got some catching up to do."

"You think?"

"Do I meet you in the lobby?"

"You'll want to go around back. The loading dock."

"Loading dock?"

"Bel's idea. She says there's a couple folks out front you don't want to meet."

"The press?"

"Bad news travels fast," he said. "We'll be fine, but if you don't want to risk it, no problemo, I can always—"

"See you in ten."

"Roger that."

We hung up, and I continued driving—heading into what, I wasn't sure. Yeshua said to do what I thought best, and he'd work it out. Alright, I was doing my part. I just hoped he'd do his.

Minutes later, I approached the courthouse and saw Sean made the right call. A TV news van was parked out front, its portable microwave dish extended a dozen feet into the air. I turned left and circled around back.

At first, I saw no one, until Sean popped out from between two garbage dumpsters. He jogged across the parking lot to join me on the street. Yanking open the door, he hopped inside and shouted, "Let's go."

"How'd they let you out back here?"

"Bel pulled some strings. Go, go." He glanced out the back window and scooted down in the seat. I pulled away, turned left at the intersection, and started for his place. Once we were clear he scooted back up.

"So tell me, what happened?" I asked.

"Not much." He snapped on the radio; the college station was playing Hayden's Symphony No. 44. He gave me a look. "Really?"

I shrugged. He scanned the stations then sighed in relief when he found some ancient Limp Bizkit. He cranked it up to just under ear-bleeding. I reached over and split the difference so we could talk. "Tell me."

"One of the sophomores in my Twentieth Century Lit class said she wasn't happy with her grade on Virginia Woolf and could she do some extra credit to bring up her score."

"And you said?"

"What did she have in mind?"

"And she said?"

"The whole structure, the interior monologue thing of *The Waves* had her confused and could we meet for coffee to discuss?"

"And you said, no." I waited, then repeated, "And you said, no."

"It was a public place, lots of people."

"Sean . . ."

"Alright, maybe I should have thought first, but come on, nobody gets *The Waves*."

"Except for the brilliant literature professor who, by the way, is unattached."

"It was at the Coffee Grinder," he argued. "The place is always packed with students."

I sighed, shaking my head.

"She had her laptop; I brought along some books. Anyone could see what we were doing."

"And?"

"We talked about Woolf, the attitude toward women at the time."

"Until . . ."

"Until it started getting personal—who was my favorite twentieth-century author? Why? And then she brings up hers."

"Who was . . ."

"Nabokov."

I groaned. "Don't tell me—"

"Yeah, *Lolita*. But I'm no idiot, right? I mean, I saw where things were going, so I try bringing the meeting to an end."

"Try?"

"It's like she doesn't hear. And, yeah, she starts talking about the attraction of older men and did I think that was wrong and how she never felt the way she felt the first day she saw me in class—and I try to gently call her on it, but she keeps going on until I finally have to shut her down. Hard."

"How'd that go?"

"What do you think?"

I shook my head. "You insensitive heart-breaker, you."

"I say goodbye, she leaves in tears, and I head for the john. That was that."

I frowned. "How can that be construed as—"

"Until I finished washing my hands and saw her standing there in the mirror."

"In the men's room?"

"The *gender-neutral* room."

I blew out my breath and swore.

"Exactly," he said. "So, she cusses me out while at the same time proclaiming her unbridled passion and accusing me of having the same feelings for her, which is clear by all the secret signs I've been sending her. I tell her she's mistaken, she breaks into more tears and races out the door. End of story."

"Except?"

"Four hours later, when the cops come banging on my door."

I could only shake my head.

"Look, I know it was stupid, okay? But she's a good kid. And she has some remarkable insights into literature."

"And older men."

"I swear to God, I never sent out any signals."

"Not even how pleased you were over her 'insights into literature'?"

"Come on, Will. Don't tell me you were never attracted to some student's passion for literature. The energy we get from those few who actually care?"

"Not outside of class."

"Alright, it was stupid. How many times do I have to say it?"

He was right, of course—about shared passions. And the joy when that rare student comes along who actually gets it. But there are some gates you never open, not even a crack, not even in your mind. Maybe those first couple years as a young professor it was rewarding and flattering to be their guide. And, yes, maybe I caught myself showing off from time to time. But once I realized the risk, I made sure those doors were locked, barred, and forever sealed.

"So," I concluded, "it's really just your word against hers."

"Except . . ."

The fact dawned on me. "Except for the witnesses who saw you coming out of the bathroom together."

"I'm not an idiot."

I figured he was doing a pretty good imitation of it but kept silent.

"After she left, I held back a minute before stepping out—"

"Into a place, 'packed with students.'"

There was no need to answer. He looked out the window as Limp Bizkit finished and Korn began, their screams filling the silence during the rest of our short drive to his place. As I mentioned, Sean and I could be polar opposites. Nothing illustrated the fact more than our living accommodations. He purchased a townhouse much closer to the action (for what it is in Bellingham)—a far cry from my hour commute to some semi-remote island in the San Juans. As we pulled onto his street, we spotted another news van. This one had the logo and call letters of a station all the way down in Seattle. Once again Sean assumed the position, scooting down out of sight.

"Just drive by," he said.

I nodded. As we passed the van I slowed, pretending to appear curious.

"Keep going," Sean hissed.

"I want to look natural."

"Then stop looking guilty."

"You want to drive?" I said, doing my best ventriloquist imitation while nodding to a passing crew member.

Once we rounded the corner, Sean slid back up in his seat.

"You're a celebrity," I said.

"Right." He thought a moment, then said, "Okay, let's go to your place. They won't look for me there."

"Uh . . ." I thought of Belinda's warning. I thought of the faculty and students who knew we were good friends. And I thought of Amber. If something went sideways, I certainly didn't want her dragged into it.

Sean caught my tone and agreed. "Right, right. Okay, drop me off here and I'll sneak in the back."

"Are you sure? Wouldn't a motel be safer?"

"They're not going to drive me out of my own house. Besides I've got my computer and papers to grade."

"Listen, partner," I said. "I may be wrong, but I'm betting work isn't going to be at the top of your list these next few days. There's a Motel 6 just down the freeway."

"Aren't you listening? I'm not going to let some college kid drive me from my own home. Pull over."

"Sean."

"Pull over."

I checked the mirrors to make sure we were clear and pulled to the curb. He climbed out and, after I promised I'd call to check in on him, he shut the door and headed for the back alley.

I sat a moment, then snapped off the radio, pointed the car toward home, and said a quiet prayer.

CHAPTER
THIRTEEN

FIRST THING SATURDAY morning, I took Siggy for a walk on the beach. Once he fell into his routine of barking, splashing, and chasing gulls, I gave Sean a call.

"You see the news?" he asked.

"Not yet. What's up?"

"I'm a star, man."

"Congratulations." It was more question than statement.

"Yeah. Her granddaddy, Benjamin Smock, the old-time rocker—did you know Juliane DiGamo was his granddaughter?"

"I don't know Juliane," I said. "And I was surprised to hear Smock was still alive."

"Exactly. Anyway, they got him on camera talking about how I destroyed her life and how my actions devastated his entire family."

I added, "Not to mention a little publicity and getting him back onto the charts."

"Don't get me started."

"Did they bring up the college?"

The line was silent.

"Sean?"

"A nice drone shot. The campus is beautiful this time of year."

I swore.

"Roger that."

"How 'bout you?" I asked. "How are you holding up?"

"Everything's fine at this end. No problemo."

"You check in with your sponsor?"

"No need. I'm clean and sober. Not a drop of booze in the house. And it's not like I'm going out shopping, not with my pals the paparazzi outside."

"Still, it wouldn't hurt to check in with him."

He snorted. "The dude's so self-righteous he'd hang up on me."

"Sean—"

"I'm serious. Pay attention to the news, bro. A gun-toting sociopath gets more sympathy these days."

"It is a new era."

"And a needed one, I get that. Seriously, I do. But tell me why I feel like some communist back in the McCarthy days. Talk about a witch hunt."

"Yeah," I agreed. "Maybe a little over-correction."

"A *little*?"

I let him rant a bit longer before we ended the call with a promise I'd check in on him later.

That had been the earlier and easiest part of my morning.

Two hours later, and for reasons I still don't entirely understand, I was in the passenger seat beside Amber, who sat behind the wheel of my beloved Honda. We had a little time to kill before Darlene arrived to prepare for tomorrow's baby shower and Amber figured it was as good a time as any to wear me down about teaching her to drive. Normally, I would have held the line, but in trying to practice Yeshua's suggestion of "deeper listening," well . . . here we were.

The first thirty minutes was spent arguing about whose car to take—her mother's Solara with the peeling paint, bad brakes, and bad transmission, or mine. On the outside, both looked equally ravaged, but when it came to dying, the chances were just slightly less in mine. I would fix her mom's car, I promised. Having an abusive father who demanded I spend an entire summer with him taking apart a car and reassembling it had its advantages. But, until I found the time, we'd be touring in my little green Honda.

Eventually, we hit the road, and for the most part, she stayed on the correct side—though it didn't stop me from practicing the Bible's edict to "Pray without ceasing." It's not that Amber was a bad driver. She was just bull-headed, had all the answers, and like everything else in life, was set on proving it.

"Why can't I use my left foot for the brake?" she argued.

"Because—" For the life of me I couldn't remember the reason and had to opt for, "that's not how it's done."

"It's just sitting there, doing nothing. Maybe somebody should tell whoever makes up the stupid rules it's time to think outside their stupid box."

"Amber—"

"That's the whole problem with this world—global warming, deforestation, carbon footprints—all because you Boomers are stuck in your stupid ways."

Before I could suggest there may be other contributing factors, she made her point by pressing the brake with her left foot, nearly throwing me through the windshield as we slid to a stop precariously close to an open ditch.

Once the screams faded (mine, not hers), I quietly pointed out, "That brake can be a little touchy."

"As if that's *my* fault."

She pulled back onto the road. It was wet and heavily shaded, with only a few shafts of sunlight filtering through a thick stand of firs. More importantly, for me and our health, it was completely deserted, not another car in sight.

I glanced at the speedometer. "Watch your speed."

"You told me to watch the road."

I sighed and looked out my window to gather patience, until I turned back to see her scooting down in the driver's seat, so low she couldn't see over the dashboard. "What are you doing?" I cried.

"Take the wheel!"

"Amber!" I grabbed the wheel as she motioned out her window to the tiny strip mall we were passing.

"That's the hottie I talked to yesterday."

"Amber, get up!"

"Is he looking?"

I glanced at the parking lot. "All I see is some pimply-face kid with greasy hair. Amber, get up."

"That's him! He's not looking over here, is he?"

"No. Slow down. Amber!"

It wasn't until another group of trees blocked us from the store's view that she slowed and slid back up.

"Why didn't you want him to see you?" I said as she took the wheel and checked herself in the mirror. "He should be impressed you're old enough to drive."

"Please," she scorned.

"What?"

"You think I want him seeing me with some old fart?"

I took a moment then responded. "You know, it wouldn't hurt if you worked a little harder to be—"

She screamed and swerved hard to the left.

"What are you—"

"Squirrel!"

"Amber!" We headed straight for a giant cedar until I lunged for the wheel and yanked us back onto the road.

"What are you doing?" she cried. "That was a squirrel!"

I checked the side mirror as it scampered safely into a bramble of blackberry bushes.

"Chipmunk," I said.

"Same diff."

"They're rodents, Amber. Squirrel, chipmunk, our lives are more important than some rodent."

"Says who?" She turned and looked out the back window. Did we hit him? Did we—"

"Brakes!" I shouted.

She spun back to see me pointing at an intersection we were fast approaching—the one another car was about to enter.

"Brakes!"

The good news was she hit the brakes. The bad news was she also hit the accelerator, blowing us through the intersection at just under fifty miles per hour, barely missing the other car. The other car that just happened to be property of the Whatcom County's Sheriff's Department.

"Stop the car!" I ordered.

The sheriff's lights lit up.

"Can we—" She glanced out the back window, panic in her voice. "Should we make a run for it?"

I looked over my shoulder to see the sheriff turning to follow.

"Stop the car," I repeated. "Pull over to the side and stop the car."

"What do we do? What do we do?"

"Stop the car!"

She hit the brakes, this time with both feet. I braced myself as we slid to a stop.

"What do we do?"

"Relax." I adjusted my side mirror to watch the car pull behind us. "Just relax, we'll be fine."

"No, we won't! How can you say that? You're not the one driving!" She was about to lift her foot from the brake to the accelerator when I quickly shoved the car into park.

"Uncle Will!"

And removed the keys.

"Uncle Will!"

"We'll be fine."

"We broke the law." Her voice trembled, tears spilling onto her cheeks. "I'm not legal. I'm underage. You should never have let me drive!"

"We'll be okay." I watched as the big man stepped from his car.

"What if they take me to jail?"

"Nobody's taking you to—"

"I can't raise my baby in jail! Uncle Will!"

❦

After a stern lecture from the officer, which Amber may or may not have heard through her tears (which may or may not have been entirely real) and a hefty fine for me (which was far too real), I drove us back to the house.

Darlene's car was parked in front of the garage where she patiently waited, wearing a snug, white ski coat, and some nicely fitted jeans.

"Hey," she called as I opened the car door which gave its customary creak and groan.

"Hey," I said, shutting it and crossing to her. "Sorry, we got hung up."

"No problem." She kept an eye on Amber who sullenly dragged herself out of the car. "Of course, it would be easier if I just had a key of my own." She forced a chuckle.

I returned it, making it clear I thought it a joke, as I unlocked the back kitchen door.

She called to Amber. "How's it going, kiddo?"

Amber arrived, head down, giving no sign of emotion. At least none I could read.

But Darlene was suddenly concerned, "Sweetheart? Amber?"

After a dramatic pause, Amber slowly looked up—eyes wet, cheeks smeared with mascara.

"Oh, sweetie." Darlene threw open her arms and Amber fell into them, a bursting dam of emotion. "What happened?"

"It was awful!" she wailed.

I pushed open the door and entered the kitchen, grateful to leave the theatrics behind. But, of course, it followed.

"What was?" Darlene said, helping her inside. "Tell me, sweetheart."

Through broken sobs, Amber retold the absolute, worst morning of her whole, absolute, entire life—as I filled a mug with water and popped it into the microwave for some instant coffee. When Amber finished, adding a few embellishments of victimhood I'd apparently missed, Darlene turned to me.

"Are you serious?" she said. "You took her out on the road?"

"Well, yeah." I cleared my throat, checking the microwave.

She cocked her head at me like I was a moron.

I countered. "You said you were going to teach her."

"Well, of course. But in the mall's parking lot, not a public street. Honestly, what were you thinking?" She turned back to Amber. "It must have been terrible."

Amber whimpered.

"I'm so sorry, sweetie."

More tears followed as Darlene looked back at me. Not exactly a glare, but close to it.

The microwave dinged and I pulled out my mug. "Coffee?"

Ignoring me, Darlene took a tissue from her coat and began dabbing Amber's face. "Well, that's all behind us now, isn't it?"

"Except the $369 fine," I mumbled as I reached into the cupboard for the Folgers.

Again, I was ignored.

"You know what?" Darlene said, "I've been shopping all morning for tomorrow's shower. Why don't you come out to the car and help me unload it?"

Amber gave another sniff and Darlene added an extra hug. "I've got a ton of things. Come on." Amber nodded and Darlene guided her toward the door. "I think we're going to have a big turnout. I've been bragging about you all week. So many people are excited to meet you. And you know, lots of people means lots of stuff."

"Cool," Amber said in a shaky breath. She swiped her face, stepping into the sunshine. And just like that, she changed gears. All trace of trauma gone. Darlene glanced over her shoulder at me with a knowing smile.

I returned it, not exactly sure what I was knowing.

They hauled in three, four, five, large paper bags (plastic ones are illegal in Washington) and unpacked them on the kitchen counter. Knowing I was expected to stay close and give positive feedback, I busied myself with the mountain of dirty dishes in the sink—rinsing and loading them into the dishwasher—a skill Amber had not yet acquired. As I figured, it wasn't long before the subject of Sean Fulton came up. I tried suggesting he had his side to the story, but since we were the same gender, I had little ground to stand on.

"I know he's your friend," Darlene said, as she dug into another bag, "but seriously, a nineteen-year-old sopho-more?" She pulled out a shrink-wrapped package of blue and pink paper plates with a stork and baby printed on them.

"Ohhh," Amber cooed, "Those are so cute, Aunt Darlene."

Aunt Darlene?

Darlene continued, "And a student of his? What was he thinking?"

"*If* he's guilty," I said.

"Oh, he's guilty."

"And you're sure of that because?"

"He's hit on me a half dozen times."

Without suggesting she wasn't exactly a poster child for chastity, I said, "By hitting on you, do you mean his actions were out of line?"

"Depends where you draw that line."

"How cool are these," Amber said, pulling out a bag of uninflated balloons crudely shaped like baby bottles.

"Was it beyond flirting?" I asked. "I mean, I know he does that. Everyone knows he does that."

Darlene stopped and simply looked at me. "Listen, Will. You're very sweet, very naïve, and a bit of a mensch."

"What's that supposed to—"

"You have no idea what it's like to be a woman. To constantly feel men's eyes leering at you, wondering what they're thinking."

Amber agreed without looking up. "Men are dogs."

"Excuse me?"

Amber continued, "All they do is objectify women."

"Um," I pointed at myself, "man here."

The two exchanged knowing looks. I didn't know what it meant, and wasn't about to ask, so I conceded, "Alright, I may be a little out of my depth here, but—"

"A little?" Darlene chuckled, then asked, "Do you have a punch bowl?"

"A punch—"

"There's one in the laundry room," Amber said. She turned for the hallway and suddenly gasped. Darlene and I traded looks. Putting her hand on her belly, Amber turned to us, grinning. "The kid's definitely going to be a soccer star." She motioned to Darlene. "Come, feel."

Darlene quickly moved to her side.

"Feel him?"

"Oh, yeah." Darlene smiled, then motioned for me to join them. I hesitated, but she insisted. "Come here."

I crossed to them, unsure what to do. Darlene took my hand and set it on Amber's bare belly—more than a little awkward—until I felt it. Movement, a flutter. The women traded looks then turned to me, no doubt seeing the awe filling my face.

"Is that . . ."

"Yes," they whispered.

Another kick. I stood in silent amazement. There were no words, just a quiet sense of wonder.

"He's coming sooner than you think," Darlene said.

"The doctor said three weeks," Amber said.

"Doctors can be wrong."

Amber straightened her blouse and turned to waddle down the hall. "I'll get the punch bowl."

As she disappeared, I asked Darlene, "Do you think she's ready?"

She looked at me.

"For the baby," I said.

"No one ever is."

"But you two have been talking, right? And she's taking classes—online, I see her watching every day."

"You think having babies is something you can learn online?"

I nodded in understanding and returned to something I knew—loading the dishwasher.

As Darlene unpacked the last of the baby shower goodies, and with Sean still very much on my mind, I asked, "Did he—did Sean ever really say or do anything, you know, inappropriate?"

"Fulton?" she said. "He didn't have to. A woman knows. We sense these things." An edge sharpened her voice. "We experience his kind of degradation every day." She folded the last bag none too gently. "And my unsolicited advice to you, my sweet, gullible friend, is stay as far away from him as possible. For your own good." Then, as quickly as it came, the edge disappeared—just as fast as

Amber's own 180-degree mood change—leaving me, once again, feeling like a visiting alien from another galaxy.

The shower preparation continued throughout the afternoon and, as I expected, on into the night. I offered to help, but my ham-fisted clumsiness quickly banished me back to grading papers in my laundry room/office. I smiled as I walked away, pleased the two weren't the only ones who knew how to play the gender game.

Later, amidst the rinse cycle of the washer and the banging tennis shoes in the dryer, I gave Sean another call. He did his best to sound chipper, but it was obvious he was wearing down.

"They're still out there, dude," he said, "only now there's two of them."

"Hang in there," I said. "It won't last forever. I'll check in with you tomorrow after church."

"Church?"

"I'm going there with Patricia Swenson."

"Patricia Swenson, the ice queen?"

"Actually, she's not that bad, once you get to know her."

He gave a quiet whistle. "Not only is our boy getting back in the game, he's aiming for the bleachers. Keep me posted, slugger."

"Likewise," I said.

FOURTEEN

"SO WHERE IS heaven? Is it up in the clouds? Past the moon? Past Jupiter?" Dr. Stewart, a fifty-something minister sat on a stool waiting for his audience to respond. He was a good-looking black man with a slight Jamaican accent and enough gray at the temples to appear scholarly. "Not Jupiter?" he said. "Then where?"

Tucked away in the historic part of the city, the coffeehouse smelled of old wood, candles, and yes, coffee. Each of the small, round tables was lit by a flickering candle with additional light provided by floor lamps along the walls and dim sunlight filtering through the closed shutters behind us. Every seat was taken, with several folks standing in back, mostly college kids. In fact, as far as I could tell, Patricia and I were the oldest in the room.

Stewart continued, "My science friends, they tease me about believing in the supernatural—you know, crazy things like angels, demons . . . God."

Quiet chuckles around the room.

"And next Sunday, come Easter, when we celebrate such an impossibility as someone rising from the dead after three days in the grave—well, it's all they can do not to snicker or break out laughing."

He paused, taking a sip of coffee. "But these friends, very good people, very brilliant, they are often the first to subscribe to the popular Superstring Theory." He waited for a response which was tepid at best. He repeated the term, more question than statement, "Superstring Theory?"

Reactions were about the same, so he went on to explain. "It is a hypothesis that the world is actually composed of the vibration of tiny, infinitesimal strings. So, my stool here, at its most fundamental level, it is not made of wood or atoms or even the subatomic particles we know of. Instead, it is made of vibrations. And what makes my stool different from, say, your tables is the frequency of its vibration. So, speaking in the most elementary terms, this stool could be a C-sharp, while your tables could be vibrating at E-flat. In essence, physical matter is no longer the building block of our universe. Instead, it is vibrations."

I noticed Patricia writing on a small notepad.

"Now if this theory is correct, and granted, theories come and go, but if it is correct, then is it possible these vibrations, instead of coming from unknown strings, is it possible these vibrations could come from—a *voice*? A spoken voice?" He turned to the cup in his hand and spoke with dramatic authority: "*COFFEE CUP!*" Then back to the group. "And, low and behold," he held it higher, "a coffee cup." He paused, letting the concept take hold. "Or if someone were to say, '*Let there be light*' and suddenly— there was light. Or, '*Let there be stars in the heavens, and creatures in the sea, and beasts of the field. And it was so.*'"

He smiled mischievously. "Your brains, are they hurting yet?"

Several shook their heads, a few murmuring no.

His smile broadened. "Good. Because there is more." He rose to his feet. "You see, for the Superstring Theory to work, physicists say the universe must consist of at least twenty-two dimensions. And if that is true, then right here, right in this room, we are surrounded by dimensions higher than we can see. We know of four, yes? Length, width, height, and the fourth, which is time. But what of the other eighteen?"

The room grew even quieter. He continued. "If those dimensions are here, why can't we see them? Maybe for the same reason we cannot see time. We know it exists, we see its effects, but we cannot reach out and physically touch it."

He took another sip of coffee. "That doesn't mean those dimensions aren't here surrounding us. They're just at a higher level, beyond what our three-dimensional senses can perceive. And yet, we have several accounts—" he turned back to his table and scooped up a small, worn Bible— "right here. Accounts of people who left their 3-D bodies and went higher. Isaiah, Ezekiel, Paul, John.

And they came back with some very freaky descriptions of those dimensions and the creatures inhabiting them— six-winged seraphim, multi-faced beings, wheels covered in eyes. All these men, their lives separated by centuries, and yet all describing the same things."

I glanced back to Patricia who was writing furiously.

"So—" he returned to his stool. "I know this is all conjecture, but what we conceivably have is a universe made up of someone's voice . . . with higher dimensions . . . inhabited by creatures we cannot see." He set down his coffee, "Call me naïve," and raised his Bible, "but haven't I just described the supernatural world mentioned in this little book?"

He shrugged. "My apologies. As Shondra says, I do go on."

A heavy-set woman up front called out, "You got that right, preacher."

More chuckles. But even as I listened, I wondered if this is what happens to me during my visits or visions or whatever. That, in some strange way, I'm slipping into some other—dimension.

Stewart continued, "Please, bear with me. There's just one more point I should like to make. One more problem for my materialist friends who only believe in what they can physically verify. Actually, two problems: dark matter and dark energy. We don't know what they are. We cannot see them. We cannot describe them, hence the term *dark*. But through careful gravitational measurements we know they exist; the facts are irrefutable. Twenty-three percent of this universe is made up of dark matter." He paused then repeated for emphasis, "*Twenty-three percent.* And when it comes to dark energy? Seventy-three percent. *Seventy-three.*"

He looked around the room. "Do you understand the significance of this? The ramifications? When added up, that means 96 percent of the reality around us cannot be observed, or even defined. *Ninety-six percent.* We have no idea what it is. We know it is here. It is all around. But that is all we know.

"So, to my friends who insist they only believe in a material world, I say, congratulations, you believe in 4 percent of reality." Holding up the Bible, he added, "If it is okay with you, I shall believe in more."

"He's good," a familiar voice said.

I looked over to see Yeshua sitting on the table between Patricia and me.

"What are you—" I caught myself, afraid of being overheard.

"It's okay," he said. "Just think the words."

I nodded and thought, "*What are you doing here?*"

"It's church. Where else would I be on a Sunday morning? So, what do you think of my man? I really like him."

"*You like everyone.*"

He shrugged. "Guilty as charged."

"Does he know what he's talking about?" I asked.

"He's pointed in the right direction. But there's a lot more to the kingdom of God than higher dimensions."

"Such as?"

"The kingdom of God is where God is king."

"Okay . . ."

Suspecting I wanted more, he continued, "Back on the hill, when I was dying for you, isn't that what you asked—for us to be your king?"

"Right . . ."

"So," he reached over and tapped my chest. "The kingdom of God is where God is King."

"Metaphorically."

He shook his head. "We've covered this, Will. The kingdom of God is within you. Your body is the temple of the Holy Spirit."

I nodded, though it was still a lot to grasp.

He looked over to Patricia who was writing up a storm, trying to capture every detail. Sadness crept over his face and he reached out to gently set his hand on her shoulder. If she felt it, she was too busy to respond.

"Is she alright?" I asked.

Still watching her, he quietly answered, "She will be. That's why you're here."

"Why I'm *here?"*

"Of course. You're helping her."

"I'm helping her?"

He turned back to me. "Did you think this is all just an accident?"

"I'm not—"

"I don't play defense, remember?"

"Right, but if anybody needs help, she *should be helping me."*

He appeared surprised.

"What?" I thought.

He smiled. "And I thought my disciples were slow." He looked down, shaking his head.

"What's that supposed to mean?"

"It means we'll talk." As he spoke, he began disappearing.

"Wait. Don't go."

He continued to dissolve, blending into the flickering candlelight.

"C'mon," I said out loud, "I need to know more. Don't go!"

Patricia turned to me quizzically—along with others in the room.

She leaned to me and quietly whispered, "We can stay after if you'd like."

"Right, uh . . ."

"I'm sure he'll be happy to answer any of your questions."

FIFTEEN

EXCEPT FOR THREE or four kids cleaning tables and packing up sound gear, the room had pretty much cleared. Our time with Dr. Stewart was short and had little to do with his sermon. Nobody's fault but mine. I mentioned we were under a time crunch with Amber's upcoming shower—and the whole conversation changed. As soon as Shondra, his wife, learned Patricia declined the invitation, had in fact never even attended one, we were off to the races, heading an entirely different direction.

"Seriously?" she asked, "You've never been to a baby shower?"

Patricia shook her head. "I have not."

"Not even one?"

"It's my understanding they're mostly frivolous affairs with gossipy women."

"Present company excluded." Stewart gave me a wink.

"Or not." I grinned.

"Besides," Patricia explained, "we have the garage sale this afternoon."

Shondra was already shaking her head. "Girl, we've been over this how many times? You got to get into other things. There's more to life than just Bible and church."

"I can't believe you're saying that," Patricia said.

"Believe it," the woman said.

Patricia replied, "The Word clearly says, 'Worship the Lord God and serve him only.'"

The big woman sighed and looked away in exasperation, muttering something clearly not in *The Minister Wife's Handbook*.

Dr. Stewart took a more tactful approach. "Patricia, sometimes life, the useless and mundane, sometimes those very things are where God dwells."

She remained respectfully silent.

He continued, "He wants a daughter, Patricia. Not a servant."

Unable to restrain herself, she fired back, "While the world is going to heck in a handbasket?"

Stewart looked down, suppressing a grin.

She continued, "'The harvest is plentiful, but the workers are few.' Matthew 9:37."

He raised his head back to her and gently replied, "My counsel to you, as your pastor, is you should go to that baby shower."

Shondra quipped, "Who knows, maybe there's somebody's soul there you can save."

Stewart shot his wife a look and she reluctantly backed down. Then, to Patricia, he repeated, "Go."

"But Will, here," she said, "he has some serious questions."

"I'm sure they can wait. Go."

She looked to me. I gave less than a helpful shrug. Finally, with a sigh, she began buttoning her coat.

"And have a big ol' helping of empty carb cake while you're at it," Shondra said, "or two."

Dr. Stewart could only look back to the ground and shake his head.

℘

"What, are you nuts?" Sean exclaimed. "The Ice Queen is heading to your house and you're coming to visit me! Where are your priorities, man?"

"I promised. You're there all by yourself with nobody to—"

"I'm fine. I've got cable, I've got porn."

"That stuff will rot your brain."

"Which?"

Earlier, Patricia and I said goodbye at the coffee shop. Under protest, she agreed to attend the baby shower. I gave her my address and explained I had a few errands to run but would try to get to the house before it was over. She was even less crazy about that idea. Still, she gave her word to her pastor, and her word was her word. Mine, on the other hand, as I spoke with Sean, seemed to be waffling.

"Don't worry about me, dude. Smoke is already clearing. The news crews are packing up even as we speak."

"Really?"

"I'm yesterday's news. Literally. Didn't you hear about the guy they caught mistreating puppies at some puppy mill in Sedro-Woolley?"

"What?"

"Gotta keep up with the times, my friend. Focus on the relevant. 'Sides, Belinda thinks the family's bitten off more than they can chew. Whole things gonna blow over in a day or two."

"They're still pressing charges."

"For now. So go. Enjoy yourself. I'll be fine."

"You sure? I'm only a few miles from your—"

"I'm sure, I'm sure. You're finally back in the game. Go for it, dude."

I took a deep breath and blew it out.

"Will?"

"Alright, alright," I said.

"Atta boy."

"But Sean?"

"Yeah?"

"Stay away from the porn."

"Hey, at least it can't sue me."

SIXTEEN

I'D NO SOONER hung up with Sean before I was sitting on one of several wooden benches surrounding a small speaker's area in the middle. The room was roughly thirty by thirty feet, the walls white plaster, the floor swept dirt. I guessed there to be fifty or so men with me, all sitting, all intently listening to Yeshua who stood in the center, reading from a scroll:

> *"The Spirit of the Lord is upon me, because he has anointed me to proclaim good news to the poor. He has sent me to proclaim freedom for the prisoners and recovery of sight for the blind, to set the oppressed free, to proclaim the year of the Lord's favor."*

He finished reading, murmured a quiet prayer I couldn't quite hear, then rolled up the scroll, kissed it, and handed it to the attendant. With every eye on him, he began to speak. "I tell you, today, in your hearing, this very scripture has been fulfilled."

If the room was quiet before, it was dead silent now. Looks were traded, brows furrowed, as everyone leaned forward to hear more.

That's when Yeshua's eyes landed on me. He broke into a gentle smile and motioned for me to join him. I glanced around the room then back to him and mouthed the words, *"Is it safe?"*

He nodded and spoke. "For you."

I rose and, as I worked my way through the men, I asked, "Are you doing that time-stop thing again?"

"Trust me," he motioned to their frozen faces, "they'll need all the time they can get to digest what I've just said."

I looked around and took a guess. "This is Nazareth again, right? Your hometown."

He smiled. "You *have* been reading. And?"

"You just quoted something about yourself out of the Old Testament."

"The prophet Isaiah, 700 years ago." Looking out to the group he added, "And I just announced my mission."

"'*To proclaim freedom for the prisoners and to those who are oppressed.*'"

He nodded. "That's right. But freedom for who? Oppressed by what?"

I took another guess. "I know politics aren't your thing, so you're *not* talking about the Romans."

"So, freedom for . . ."

I motioned to the men. "Well, for them."

He gave another nod. "And for your friend."

"Sean."

"No. The woman."

"Patricia?"

"I said you'd help her, remember?"

"Right. But why Patricia and not Sean?"

"Slavery is slavery."

"I don't understand. Everything she does is good. She's like your perfect Christian."

"She's as much a captive as your friend."

"Uh, no," I said. "Sean's got a dozen issues."

"Issues?"

"Like—well, we were just talking about his porn."

"It's all the same."

"What?" I tried not to laugh. "How are porn and Patricia's problems the same?"

"Porn is his prison. It's the counterfeit pleasures of his flesh enslaving him, preventing him from the deeper commitment of his heart."

I slowly nodded. "Okay," then added, "And don't forget it objectifies and uses women."

"Just as religion, when misused, objectifies and uses me."

"What?"

"The flesh will do anything to avoid the heart's deeper commitment to me. Even become religious."

I frowned, trying to understand. "But, Patricia, she's good and decent and righteous. And Sean is . . ."

"Do you love him?"

"Of course, but—"

"Do you think your love for him is greater than mine?"

"No, but Patricia—"

"Is bound up in fear. She keeps trying to prove her love for me, instead of resting and letting me love her."

"We're *supposed* to love you," I argued. "'*Love the Lord your God with all your heart, soul and mind.*'"

"How's that working for you?"

"I . . . try."

"And?"

I wanted to lie, but given who I was speaking to, I settled for a slumping shrug.

"Exactly," he said. "You can't. Not on your own. So people force it. Out of fear. Or obligation." He cocked his head at me and asked, "How does one love out of fear and obligation?"

I had no answer.

"They can't," he said. "They can only get religious. And religion can become love's counterfeit." I started to disagree but he cut me off. "When they fail, they're full of guilt. When they succeed, they're full of pride. The truth is, I'm the author of real love. You can only love me with the love I've first given you."

"So . . . we can't even love you on our own?"

"Appreciate, maybe. But authentic love can only come from me."

I stared at the ground, trying to understand.

"Your friend needs to stop running and be still. She needs to stop striving to be religious and simply soak in my presence. She needs to stop *doing* and start *abiding*."

"While the rest of the world goes to *heck in a handbasket*?"

He didn't smile at my attempted humor. Instead, he replied, "The fruit she wants to bear can only come when she rests in me."

"'*Be still, and know I'm God*,'" I said. "We talked about that. But how does being still accomplish anything? How would we get anything done for you?"

"You're only quoting half the verse."

"There's more?"

He closed his eyes and softly quoted. "'*Be still, and know I am God; I will be exalted among the nations; I will be exalted in the earth*.'"

When he opened his eyes he saw my jaw slacked at the obvious paradox. "How is that possible?" I asked.

"If she's serious about exalting me, she has to be still and '*know*' me."

"But—"

"If she rests and soaks in my presence, I'll not only fill her, but spill out of her onto others. From her heart will flow rivers of living water."

I paused, trying to unpack all I heard. But he still wasn't finished.

"Like your niece, Patricia is an adolescent in the kingdom of God. She thinks she has to prove herself, that she has to do it all on her own. And, just like your niece, you can help her grow into adulthood until she's no longer barren and begins giving birth."

"Birth—as in spiritual children, right?"

He smiled. If he knew more, he wasn't telling.

I took a deep breath and blew it out. "That's a lot to digest," I said.

He motioned to the men, "No more than what they're about to hear."

"You're not finished?"

He looked back to them and took a breath of his own. "I've just begun."

I turned to scan the faces. "They don't look happy."

He sadly nodded. "Religion dies hard."

CHAPTER

SEVENTEEN

"YOU'VE NEVER DIAPERED a baby before?" Darlene asked.

With one hand held behind her back, Patricia looked up from the baby doll she was struggling to diaper. "It's just, it's been a very long, that is to say . . ." She was no good at lying—we all suspected from lack of practice.

Darlene continued to gently goad. "I can understand no children—"

One of the women quipped, "Some girls have all the luck." Others chuckled.

"—but no nieces or nephews?"

Patricia shook her head, continuing to struggle while turning to me. "I need another safety pin."

As her other hand in the contest, I answered, "Um, I think three is enough for that side."

No chuckles this time, just secret smiles. The dozen women surrounding us weren't exactly mean, at least according to my definition. Then again, we've already established my inability to read the opposite sex. It's true, the rest of the group had finished the game long ago and now stood around simply watching the entertainment. As a man, I was given the benefit of the doubt, some even considering my inexperience cute. I can't say they offered the same grace to Patricia.

It may have started when she arrived late, having first swung by a toy store to pick up a present.

Amber had simply stared at it, dumbfounded. "A tricycle? You bought my baby a tricycle?"

Patricia smiled, producing yet another gift. "And a helmet."

A half dozen expressions simultaneously crossed Amber's face.

Darlene swooped in for the rescue. "That's so sweet, Patty. Really." Then to the others, "I mean, who would have the foresight to think of something so far ahead? Right, ladies?"

The women nodded with earnest replies and more smiles.

Now it's true, Patricia could have worked a little harder to fit in—like joining in toasts for the baby and mother-to-be. But that would involve a glass of wine, or at least a diet soda. She consumed neither alcohol nor carcinogens.

But Darlene, eyes growing glassier by the drink, was always there to help. "I'd offer you some water, Patty, but

I don't know if it's filtered. Is it, Will? Is your water pure enough for her to drink?"

"I'm fine," Patricia coolly replied.

"I'm sure you are, sweetheart." Darlene grinned. "I'm sure you're just perfect."

A couple women had the good sense to subtly move between them. I, on the other hand, made a point to stay at Patricia's side throughout the party—not only to protect her from those smiles, but because nothing bonds a couple like mutual suffering. It's not that I hated the experience. Why wouldn't I love hanging with the girls, mostly faculty members, sharing baby stories, baby gifts, and baby diaper surprises, not to mention the humorous breast-feeding malfunctions and various body reconfigurations. I know I'm sounding sexist—again. And yes, I realize it's trendy for today's dads to attend baby showers—though it's not my fault they haven't the experience to come up with viable excuses. Give them time, they'll learn.

I found myself equally unqualified for the games. Wearing clothes pins you have to give up each time you said the word "baby"? Of course, I came in last place. Seriously, why wouldn't you talk about the one thing the entire gathering is about? However, I did manage to win one contest: The "Who Knows Most About the Mother-To-Be Game." A slam dunk since I'd known Amber all fourteen of her years, while everyone else, except Darlene, was going on three hours. Even at that, Darlene and I nearly tied—a telling indictment, since the two had only known each other since Christmas. Still, a win was a win. (What I'd do with a rosewood-scented candle for a prize was anybody's guess.)

And our guest of honor—the terrified, know-it-all, half-woman/half-child? Within minutes, she began a softening I'd never seen before. And, soon I began to understand why Darlene thought a baby shower was so necessary. Amber lived months, in some ways years, without a mother's influence. Now she had a dozen of them, loving and fawning over her, their maternal instincts on steroids—as she listened, wide-eyed to their anecdotes, learning to laugh with them, to enjoy the teasing, and to tease back. I stood off to the side, moved by the transformation. She had been deprived of so much. And no effort of mine could provide the comfort or sustenance to nourish that part of her soul which had slowly been starving to death.

Finally, there was the reveal. Amber had been adamant about not knowing the gender of the child until birth. But Darlene insisted it was necessary, at least in these last few weeks, so we could prepare. For the record, I'd invested more than a few prayers stacking the deck in favor of a boy, somebody I could actually relate to. And, to his credit, God delivered. The reveal was a simple procedure. Amber popped one balloon after another over her head. And when the right balloon finally burst, it covered her with light, blue powder. For the first time in my life, I saw my niece break into legitimate, heartfelt sobs. As much as I wanted to be there for her, I held no grudge when she threw herself into Darlene's arms.

I turned to Patricia. "Is she okay?" I asked. "She said she wanted a boy, so why is she—"

"She's fine," Patricia whispered. I started for her but Patricia gently took my arm. "She's okay, Will." She nodded toward Darlene and the others swooping in. "She'll be just fine."

Forty-five minutes later, as things began winding down and the guests prepared to catch the last ferry back to the mainland, Lexi, a younger prof from the music department, shouted over the group. "Check it out!" She motioned to her phone. "Juliane DiGamo, Fulton's victim, she just made a statement to the press."

Every person in the room pulled out their phones, and Patricia was no exception. I moved closer to watch as she connected to the video link—an attorney standing on one side, family members including Benjamin Smock standing on the other—as Juliane, trembling, never looking up from her written statement, read:

"—nor am I expecting sympathy. In my naïve, trusting innocence, I may have even brought some of this upon myself." She took a shaky breath and continued. "But I am speaking up in the name of justice. I am speaking for all the women who—I am speaking for all the other women who need the courage to stand." She swallowed. "This must not be a time for selfish weakness, but—"

"Hashtag Fulton," someone called from across the room.

Patricia, like the others, logged off the video and onto the site. I watched as hate-tweets filled her screen. She refreshed the page to find more. The kinder ones simply read "so sad" or "disgusting." Others were more explicit, suggesting lifetime imprisonment where Sean's regular showers would provide regular abuse. Before I finished, Patricia refreshed the page for the next batch. And then the next—a digital mob growing in its demand for a lynching.

PART THREE

CHAPTER
EIGHTEEN

SUNLIGHT CUT BRIGHT and low into the car. I set my cell on the seat and pulled the visor to the driver's side window blocking some of the glare. For the past fifty minutes I'd been trying to reach Sean with no success. Now I was heading north on I-5, my mind roiling with indecision—and fear and worry and guilt and, well, you name it.

Earlier, at my place, as the flood of tweets poured in, I stepped into the hallway, out of earshot of the others, and made the first of my failed attempts to call him. I'd barely disconnected when Darlene came down the hall and outed me.

"Who was that?" she asked.

"Uh . . ."

"You weren't calling Fulton?"

I started to open my mouth, but knew my second response would be as lame as my first.

She shook her head. "Unbelievable. Look, I get that he's your friend, but—"

"He's not picking up," I said. "His mailbox is full."

"Now there's a surprise."

"He needs," I swallowed back the concern, "I think he needs somebody to check in on him."

She looked at me in disbelief. "You? Are you kidding me?"

I held her gaze.

"Here," she said, "give me your hand."

I hesitated then reached out for her to take it. Without a word, she led me back into the living room, now strangely quiet with everyone texting and reading texts. "What do you see?" she asked.

"A feeding frenzy," I said.

"And for good reason."

I lowered my voice. "But he's innocent."

She simply looked at me. Then, motioning to the group, she said, "Statistically, one out of four of us were sexually abused before we turned eighteen."

I blinked. I knew the numbers were high but not that high.

She continued. "One in five of us will be raped at some point in our lifetime. And you think this is unjustified?"

"I—" Still trying to absorb the facts, I answered, "I'm not minimalizing that. I just—he's innocent, he's my friend, and he's out there all by himself."

"And you're the white knight that's going to rescue him."

"If I don't, who will?"

She shook her head. "You're a fool."

"I've been called worse."

"And you will be."

"I know, I know, but—"

"The school. Your reputation." She sighed with an oath and added, "Your whole future in academics is at risk."

"Only if he's guilty."

Another oath, this time louder.

I waited a moment, then asked, "Listen, can you, is there any chance of you spending the night?"

She gave me another look.

"Someone should stay with Amber," I said.

"I'll not be your accomplice."

"If I can get him by phone, I promise I'll turn around and come right back. Nobody will know."

"And if you can't?"

There was no need to answer and she knew it. Nodding across the room, she said, "Why don't you ask Patricia over there? Oh, let me guess. What would Snow White think of you hanging out with a sexual predator."

"He's not a—"

She waved me off. "Whatever."

I waited, making it clear I needed an answer. She stewed a moment then replied, "Alright. Fine."

"Thanks." I turned and headed back down the hall to get my coat. "I owe you."

"I'll put it on your tab."

Once I grabbed my coat and keys, I took the garage exit, but not before telling Patricia there was an emergency—which wasn't exactly a lie. And I didn't feel bad about abandoning her, either, now that she had joined the tweeter sisterhood.

"Seventy-nine, huh?" Yeshua's words jarred me from my thoughts. I turned and was surprised to see him leaning toward me from the passenger seat, checking the speedometer. Regaining my composure, I answered, "What? Now you're a legalist?"

He sat back in his seat and smiled. "It's not the speed limit I'm talking about." He reached into the folds of his robe and pulled out a deflated balloon similar to what I gave him in Galilee back at one of our earlier meetings.

"Really?" I said. "Another teaching moment?"

"Lots of great metaphors with this thing. Of course, I can't use them on the boys back home. They'd freak at the sight of them. But you—" he took a breath and began blowing it up.

Remembering our last conversation about them, I asked, "More on temptation?"

He shook his head, finished inflating the balloon and tied it off. "It's good for any kind of outside pressure. Including—" He pressed his index finger into the balloon and let it push back.

"Worry?" I ventured. "Confusion? Concern?" I looked to the road and continued with a shade of irony, "And all I have to do is ask for help."

"Nope." I turned to him and he replied, "All you have to do is connect."

"That's what I said, pray."

"I'm talking about worship."

"Worship? Now? In this mess?"

"You can rest in any situation by connecting with us through worship."

"That's absurd."

"How so?"

"I'm supposed to worship you for what's going on?"

"Absolutely not."

"Then . . ."

"Worship us in the *midst* of the situation, not because of it. Big difference. And if you do, I guarantee in five, ten, twenty minutes, our peace will always overtake your circumstance." I started to answer, but he cut me off. "*Always.*"

"What if I can't?"

"It's not a matter of can't, Will. It's a matter of won't."

"That's being hypocritical—thanking you if I don't feel like it."

"No. Being hypocritical is allowing your feelings to direct your thoughts instead of my truth."

He gazed out the windshield a moment, letting me chew on what he said. When he finally spoke, it seemed to be an entirely different subject. "Beautiful, isn't it? How the low angle sun brings out the textures of everything—the hillside, the bark of the trees, even those roadside bushes."

"He's my best friend," I said.

"Mine too."

"You say that about everyone."

"God is love."

I blew out a breath of frustration. "What if the press comes back; all those media people?"

"I like them too."

I worked to keep my voice even. "What I mean is, do I just drive up to his house, walk past them and knock on his door?"

"Is that what you want?"

"What about the school? My job?"

He continued to look out the window.

"Everyone would hate me. Amber, Patricia, Darlene. And the administration, I'm already on thin ice with them."

He reached over to the radio. "Do you mind?"

I sighed, "Why not."

He turned it on. The college station was playing Brahms, Symphony No. 2. He settled back into the seat, making himself comfortable and listened—appearing to have no intention of answering my question. When I could stand no more, I said, "I need a little help here, okay? I'm going to be there in twenty minutes. Do I go, do I not go?" I stole a look at him. His eyes were shut, lost in the music. "It's a simple question," I said. "I need a simple answer."

"Binary. You're thinking binary again. Either, or. Yes, no. When the answer is really—"

"Oranges, I know. You're multidimensional, we've covered that. But it doesn't help me with the here and now."

With eyes still closed, he answered, "You're not interested in the here and now."

"Of course I am."

"Nope."

I bit my tongue, knowing there was more.

"You're always living in the future, Will. Or in the past. You're always worrying about what has happened, which, if you've noticed, you can do nothing about—or fretting about what will happen, most of which never occurs."

"Alright," I said. "Maybe I overthink a little." He opened one eye at me. "Okay," I admitted, "a lot."

"You're so worried about the future or preoccupied with the past you've forgotten how to enjoy us in the now."

"That's not true," I argued. Then softened. "Is it?"

He sat up. "Do you want to play a game?"

"Come on," I said. "I'm being serious here."

"And I'm not?"

"We'll be there in fifteen minutes."

"It's called, *Now*. Here are the rules. Are you ready for the rules?"

I sighed in resignation. "Alright."

"Rule number one: you can't worry about the future."

"Got it."

"Rule number two: you can't dwell on the . . ." He looked at me and I finished.

"The past. Is this really necessary?" I asked.

"More than you know. Are you ready?"

I sighed wearily. When he got this way, there was no reasoning with him. "Okay," I said.

"Terrific." He settled back into the seat and began. "So, what are you experiencing right now, in the moment?"

"Besides frustration?"

"Good, that's good. What else?"

I frowned, trying to think of something.

"What do you see? With your eyes?"

I scanned the road, the embankment beside us. "That giant pine tree off to the right."

"And? Come on, Will, you're a word guy."

"Alright," I said. "I see wet pine needles—shimmering silver from the recent rain."

"Very good. And?"

"And—" I gave another sigh, waiting for something to come to mind. "And it reminds me when I was a little boy, how my sister and I used to climb the old—"

He cleared his throat and I looked over to him. "Just the tree, Will. Just the now."

"Right," I said. "Because we're about to pass it and I won't be able to see it and—" He was shaking his head and I came to another stop. "I'm doing it again, aren't I?"

"Just the now." Looking to the tree, he quietly marveled, "We do good work, don't we?"

"Yes," I admitted, "you do."

"You're welcome."

I turned to him. "Excuse me? I didn't—"

"That was worship."

"But I—I didn't say anything."

He smiled and closed his eyes, continuing to listen to the radio. "Brahms, right?"

"Yes," I said. We sat in the quiet with nothing but the hum of tires and gentle, aching cellos answered by the higher strings.

As we listened, I quietly mused, "I remember the first time I heard this. The Seattle Symphony, my second date with Cindy. We got into such a fight. I thought for sure we'd—" This time I caught myself. "Sorry. The past, right?"

He nodded to the radio. "I love this part." We sat there, simply enjoying the music for a long moment, before he finally threw me a smile. "Feeling better?"

"A little."

It takes practice, but with patience, you can always enjoy us in the now. "'Patience,'" I quoted from some text I'd read. "'Enduring the moment to reach a goal.'"

"No," he said. "*Enjoying* the moment, to experience us now." I understood and slowly nodded. He continued. "Look around you, Will. Everything you see is now." He motioned out the windshield, then to the sun-cracked vinyl of the dashboard, then the coffee stain on the console. "There's so much here. Why fill your head with worries about a future that may never come, or a past you can never fix? When, right here, we're surrounding you on all sides with our goodness, with our eternal now."

It was a lot to digest, but I think I actually started to get it—at least for a moment. Until my frustration returned. "That still doesn't change what I'm supposed to do about Sean," I said. "There are a dozen things that can go wrong, go sideways, and I don't—"

Suddenly the car stopped. I wasn't thrown forward. Just, one minute we were moving, the next not. I looked out the window. We sat across the street from Sean's townhouse. Directly in front of it were parked two news vans.

"Wait," I cried, "what happened? We had another ten minutes left?"

"I know," he sighed, "and there's so much we could enjoy together. But if you're set on wasting the now by worrying about the future, we might as well go there."

"But . . ." I looked across the street where two camera crews were resetting their equipment back on Sean's front lawn, a dozen feet from his door. "What do I do when I pass them? What do I say when I go to the front door?"

He cocked his head at me. "You're really not very good at this, are you?"

"But—"

"Keep practicing, my friend."

And then he was gone.

"Wait!" I protested. "C'mon! I need you. Now, more than ever!"

And then, whether it was his voice or my imagination, I'm not sure, but a phrase bubbled up in my mind: "We've had the lecture, Will. Now it's time for the lab."

NINETEEN

I TOOK A deep breath while watching the news crews through my window. They were too busy setting up to notice me. Of course, that was about to change.

I removed my keys and stepped outside where I stood a moment. The sun had just dropped out of sight and darkness was coming fast. I took another breath, muttered some type of prayer and/or complaint, and headed across the street. I stepped between the two vans and came upon a thirty-something blonde finishing her smoke. We exchanged nods and I continued forward. It wasn't until I started up the sidewalk for the front steps, did anyone take notice.

"Excuse me," a man called from behind. "Sir?"

I didn't turn.

"Sir?" It was a woman's voice. I suspected the blonde's.

I breathed faster, facing forward, keeping my head down.

"Sir?"

By the time I reached the porch, my heart pounded in my ears. I started up the steps, all five of them. I heard commotion and scrambling behind me but never turned to look.

"Sir, do you know Sean Fulton? Are you a friend? A relative?"

I reached the screen door and pressed the bell. If it worked, I didn't hear.

"Sir?"

I pulled open the screen and knocked.

Another voice joined in. "Are you part of his legal team?"

Lights flared on behind me. First one, then another. But it made no difference. If they wanted a better view of my back, they had it. The point is, I'd passed through the gauntlet without them seeing my face or being recognized.

"Sir? Excuse me! Sir!"

A curtain from the living room window parted then closed. I waited, almost smiling. It was exactly as Yeshua said. My worries far exceeded any reality. Or so I thought. The front door opened, and Sean appeared—hair disheveled, bathrobe half-open. And drunk.

"Will!" he shouted as he pushed open the screen. "Will Thomas! Thank God you're here!"

At work, Sean always dressed impeccably—a bow tie for every occasion, the latest cut in pants, and his shirts or sweaters always snug enough to indicate his frequent visits to the gym. "Never hurts to advertise," he was fond of saying. He was equally meticulous about his townhouse. That's why I was taken aback by what greeted me—not only by his choice of wardrobe but by the pizza boxes, dirty plates, empty beer cans, and two-thirds empty bottle of Seagram's 7 on the coffee table. The leather sofa sported a pile of laundry and scattered fast-food wrappers. And the smell? Let's just say it matched the decor.

"Boy, it's good to see you!" he shouted over the TV blaring from across the room. He moved unsteadily to the sofa where he shoved aside the clothes and clutter. "Sit, sit."

"I like what you've done with the place," I said.

"What?"

"The place!" I yelled over the TV. "Who's your decorator?"

He laughed and I sat, pulling an empty beer can from between the cushions. Motioning to it, I said, "I thought you couldn't get out?"

"BevMo!" he shouted. "They deliver."

I nodded at the pizza boxes. "And Domino's."

"Canadian Bacon and pineapple!" He collapsed, sprawling out on the sofa. "Man, is it good to see you."

I motioned to the TV. "Any chance we could, uh . . ."

"Oh, right, right." Struggling to sit up, he searched for the remote amidst the trash on the table and accidentally knocked over the open bottle of Seagram's. Swearing, he quickly righted it and grabbed a sweatshirt to mop it up— while knocking over several empties in the process. "Sorry, man," he said. "I'm so sorry."

I found the remote, squinted at the two dozen buttons and spotted what might be *mute.* I hit it and was met with blessed silence—except for the mopping and clinking cans. And his muttering—"Stupid, stupid, stupid." It was a small spill, but he just kept mopping. "Sorry, dude. Stupid! I'm so sorry."

The emotion made me uncomfortable. Fortunately, there was a car insurance commercial to focus on—until, without warning, he angrily swiped the rest of the cans to the floor. Then the pizza boxes. Before I could respond, he changed gears and, as if nothing happened, asked, "Can I get you anything? Pizza?"

I shook my head.

"You sure? A drink?"

"I'm good."

He threw back his head on the sofa and shouted at the ceiling. "I should have known!"

I started to answer but chose to wait.

A moment later he covered his face and began to quietly sob, "I'm sorry—so sorry . . .." His voice thickened. "Stupid—stupid—stupid!"

Of course, it was the booze talking, but it was also the truth. And as bad as I felt for him, I was also angry. Real angry. He'd not only destroyed his own reputation, but he'd put the school in jeopardy. And me. How could he have been so unthinking? So selfish? Did I want to tear into him? You bet. But there was little room to squeeze in my anger between all his self-loathing.

He pressed the heel of his palms against his eyes. "I didn't do anything! I swear to God. I know the boundaries. I'd never do that." He looked to me, eyes moist and red. "You believe me, right? Right?"

I gave a curt nod.

"I'm a respected college professor! Why won't anybody believe me?"

I sat quietly as he writhed and carried on—sometimes in self-pity, but mostly self-hatred. I felt no need to join in. As I said, he was beating up himself enough for both of us. So, I just sat, staring at the TV, sometimes nodding, hoping my presence would at least assure him he wasn't alone.

Eventually, he wore himself out and leaned back into the sofa where he closed his eyes and in due time began breathing heavily.

How long we sat like that, I don't know. But we were well into some home remodeling show when he suddenly sat up and wiped his face. Sounding like himself, though still three sheets to the wind, he said, "It looks like we missed the news."

"I'm sorry?" I said.

He reached for the remote. "Don't worry, I've recorded it."

"Is that really such a good—"

He surfed the channels then stopped. "Ah, here we go."

CHAPTER
TWENTY

THE REPORT WAS brutal—beginning with DiGamo's news conference.

"I am not looking for retribution," Juliane said, appearing even more frail on the big screen. "Nor am I expecting sympathy."

"Just a way to destroy my life!" Sean yelled. "And get Gramps back on the charts!"

I leaned forward, trying to hear as she continued. "In my naïve, trusting innocence, I—

"Innocence my—"

"Shh," I motioned him to chill.

"I am speaking up for all the other women who need the courage to stand."

"Courage!" Sean struggled to his feet, shouting oaths until his photo appeared on the screen. "What the— who gave them— where did they get that?"

Now a reporter, the same one I saw outside the house, stood at the south entrance of our campus interviewing a senior we both recognized.

"That's Denise Booker!" Sean cried. "She's in my comp class. Why would she—"

Again, I motioned him to be quiet, and again he ignored me.

"I thought she liked me!"

Next up, another student—some chunky jock I never met, suggesting specific portions of Sean's reproductive system be removed. Sean erupted in a tirade so loud the outside reporters didn't need to come inside for a quote. Other scenes followed, including the university's President Sydow insisting the school "takes such accusations very seriously" and, from what I was able to hear, "planning on launching our own investigation." He was followed by a group of students talking about some rally, with the report finally ending by returning to the newswoman for a recap.

And it was over. Less than ninety seconds to destroy a life and malign a university. For what it's worth, I was grateful they didn't have time to include my lighted backside as part of the story.

"Guilty until proven innocent!" Sean shouted. Somewhere he found another beer as he took center stage between me and the TV. "We're back in the '50s, dude! Joseph McCarthy all over again. Everyone's shaking in their boots! Afraid we'll be found out!"

"Found out for . . . ?"

"Being men!"

"I don't think that's what they're—"

"Okay, I'm a man! Guilty as charged!" He started for the curtained windows, shouting at those outside. "Throw me in prison! Castrate me 'cause I'm a man! God forbid I'm a red-blooded male who likes females!"

"Sean." I rose, fearing he'd throw open the curtains to continue the show.

"Oh, I like women?" he yelled. "Guilty! Oh, I flirt with them? Guilty! Like they don't flirt with me!" I reached for his arm and he yanked it away. "It's okay to strut around with skirts up to your crotch—or those skin-tight legging things. Leggings!" He swore. "Why bother to wear clothes? Just grab some spray paint!"

"Sean—"

"A can of spray paint so we don't miss anything! And God forbid I take a second look, 'cause I'm sure, oh so sure, you didn't have that in mind. Parade around us like whores and then whine because we—"

"Sean!" I grabbed him and he turned to me.

"And you! Mr. Jesus freak, the hypocrite. Don't tell me you don't look. I've seen you. He ain't made you a eunuch, has he? Not yet?"

"Come on," I said. "Sit down and—"

"Leave me alone!" He jerked his arm free. "Who asked you to come here anyway? What do you know about women? Nothing! You got one throwing herself at you, begging for it and you ignore her for some frigid ice queen! What's with you, Thomas? Run out of testosterone?"

The cell in my back pocket started to ring.

"No wonder Cindy left you. She wanted a real man!"

A low blow I blamed on the booze. My cell continued ringing.

Hearing it, he shouted, "Answer it! Maybe it's some hot nun!"

I reached for my phone and glanced at its screen.

"Some priest with his little boy!"

I hesitated, not recognizing the number.

"And they call *me* a pervert! Answer it! Answer your phone!"

I hit receive and said, "Hello?"

"Is this Will Thomas?" the voice asked.

"Who's this?"

"Will Thomas, professor at Western Washington University?"

"Who's—"

"Dr. Thomas, I'm Stephanie Miller from the *Everett Chronicle*. One of our reporters just saw you enter—"

"Is that Darlene?" Sean yelled. Without waiting for an answer, he shouted, "Come on over, sweetheart, let's party!"

"Is that Sean Fulton," the voice asked. "Are you with him now?"

I looked at him. "Uh, no, I—"

"Give that to me." He reached for the phone but I turned blocking him as I disconnected.

He spun back to the curtained window and bellowed, "It's all rigged! I've done nothing wrong. I'm innocent! INNOCENT!" He turned back on me. "Tell me one thing, name one thing I've done wrong."

"We all make mistakes."

"It was not a mistake!"

"C'mon, dude," I said. "You know you never should have—"

"Whose side are you on?"

"Yours, of course. But you've got to face the facts or you'll never—"

He threw his arms toward the window. "You're no better than they are!"

"Why? 'Cause I'm saying you're not totally blameless?"

He stared at me, mouth ajar.

"I'm just saying—"

"Get out." His voice was low and quivering.

"All I'm saying is there are some realities you have to—"

"Get out!"

"Sean—"

"I said get out!"

"I'm on your side, but—"

He started toward me. "Now!"

I held my ground. "I'm not leaving you. Not when you're—"

He got in my face and roared. "I said, get out!" He gave me a push.

"I'm not—"

He pushed again, so hard I stumbled backward. "Get out now!"

"I—"

He stormed at me again, eyes filled with such rage I thought he'd take a swing. "Now!"

I held up a hand. "Alright. Alright!" There was no way to reason with him. "But I'll be back."

"Go!"

"But you have to promise me, you won't—"

"Don't tell me what to do!" He stalked toward the door. "Get out!" He grabbed the handle. "Now!"

I held his look a moment—his eyes on fire, his chest heaving.

"I'll be—"

"Now!" He yanked open the door.

I hesitated then stepped outside. And before I could turn, the door slammed behind me—as lights from the news crews came on.

"Dr. Thomas, Dr. Thomas, how is he?"

I saw no faces, only glaring light.

"Why are you here? Do you have a statement?"

I raised a hand, shielding my eyes. "A statement? No, I—" Thinking better than to continue, I shook my head and started down the steps.

"Surely you've got something to say?" It was the woman reporter.

Another added, "In your own defense."

I slowed to a stop. "In *my* defense? You're the ones destroying a man's life and you want *me* to defend *my*self?"

"We're here to report a story," the woman said. "Why are *you*?"

"Report?" I knew I should shut up, but I couldn't. "You're not reporting. You're carrying out the sentence. You've tried him, found him guilty, and now—"

"He's been accused of sexually assaulting a student."

I heard my phone ringing again and ignored it. "Yes," I said, "by one person. One person who may not be as innocent as you all think."

"What does that mean?" another asked. "What are you saying?"

The phone continued to ring. "What I'm saying is there are extraneous circumstances you haven't even bothered to—"

"Are you saying she brought this on herself?"

I answered, "Things aren't always as they appear."

The phone continued.

"Are you saying she asked to be raped?"

I opened my mouth but this time had the good sense to stop. Without further word, I pushed past them and continued down the sidewalk.

"Dr. Thomas . . . Dr. Thomas . . ."

I moved between the vans and crossed the street to the safety of my car. I'd barely entered before the lights arrived, blasting through my window. I reached over to lock my door, then turned on the ignition. As I dropped into gear, one of the cameramen tried to play chicken until I inched forward making it clear I wasn't stopping. He moved aside and I headed down the street, lights glaring through my rear window . . . as my phone continued to ring.

TWENTY-ONE

BECAUSE MY PARTICULAR ferry doesn't run in the middle of the night, I grabbed a cheap motel room. The mailbox for my phone was full—mostly with numbers I didn't recognize. Now, early morning, as I lay in bed deleting them, I ran across one I did know. I quickly hit 'dial'.

"Hi, Darlene."

"Will?"

"How's it going? How's Amber?"

"Alright—considering."

"Considering?"

"Where are you?"

"A motel, just off the—"

"Do you really think Juliane DiGamo asked to be raped?"

"What?"

She quoted, "'*Not as innocent as you think? Things aren't as they appear?*'"

I sat up. "What are you talking about?"

"You haven't checked the news?"

The room rumbled from another passing semi as I looked to the untouched remote near the TV.

"Do you really believe that?" she asked.

"No, I—well, yes, but—not like that."

Her silence was deafening.

"It's on the news?" I asked.

"Every local morning show."

"I—" Throwing off the covers, I rose to my feet. "And Amber?"

"She's the one who told me. Says she can't ever show her face in public again. Where'd you say you were staying?"

I paced barefoot in front of the bed, lit by the glow of parking lot lights filtered through old, yellowed sheers. "Some motel just off the 5."

"You might want to stay there for a while."

"What? Why? I've got classes."

"Some of the kids, they're organizing a rally."

"Against Sean?"

"—and you."

I opened my mouth but no words came.

She continued, "I've got class this morning. You're good with Amber staying here by herself?"

"During the day, sure, no problem."

More silence.

"Darlene?"

She finally answered, "All right then. I'll say my good-byes to her before I leave. But remind her it has nothing to do with her, okay? I'm going to miss her; she needs to know that."

"What are you saying? Darlene?"

"We're done, Will. At least for now."

"Wha—"

"You can drop her off for a visit any time she wants, but right now I really don't want to see you."

"Dar—"

"I don't want you to call me either. Is that clear?"

"You can't be—"

"Is that clear?"

I leaned against the wall. "If you'd just let me explain."

"Some other time."

"But—"

"Goodbye, Will. And—good luck."

"Darlene."

The line went dead. Another semi thundered past as I stood there, trying to absorb what just happened. I hit speed dial to call Amber. The phone rang four times before going to voice mail:

"Hi. You know the drill." *Beep.*

I hung up and tried again. Her phone rang only once before I was cut off. I redialed Darlene, hoping she could convince Amber to pick up.

After four rings hers also kicked into voice mail.

☙

It was cold and drizzly as I drove up I-5. Fog enshrouded the freeway like thick, dirty cotton. I tried calling Darlene and Amber a half dozen times. The results were always the same. Amber showed me how to block certain numbers. I suspected that's what she did with mine. Darlene, too. I even tried Patricia but, for whatever reason, she didn't pick up. And, yes, I turned on the motel's TV in hopes and fear of seeing myself. And I was not disappointed. There I was in all my vain stupidity, squinting against the lights—a middle-aged man having the audacity to lecture the new world order on how to treat sexual assault—*alleged* sexual assault.

But I could not, I would not hide. With only a few days before spring break, it was important I go back to the college and reclaim what cred I had left. Over the semester, I spent untold hours with my students. They knew me. And the students before them. And those before them. After all these years, my reputation had to count for something.

And Sean? I couldn't entirely write off his behavior to the booze. He was drunk, but not that drunk. Still, he was under incredible pressure. When the dust settled, we'd patch things up. Or, in true guy fashion, never mention it again. As I said earlier, men my age are lucky to have one or two close friends. With Sean gone, I'd be down to zero.

I rolled my head, stretching tendons in the back of my neck that had once again tightened into steel cables. That's when I heard the people—lots of them. There was nothing outside my car except the *whoosh* of passing traffic and the *swish-thump* of my wipers. I closed my eyes, reopened them, and was standing in a crowd I recognized as first-century peasants. Men, women, and children all squeezed along a narrow cobblestone street, cheering, and craning their necks. Parents setting children on their shoulders for a better view. Many waving palm branches with long, serrated fronds. Some even laid their robes and shawls on the pavement—all in celebration of the man riding a donkey.

If Yeshua saw me, he didn't let on. But I was in no mood to be ignored. I pushed through the crowd, staying parallel with him as he moved up the street. It wasn't until we reached the entrance to a large, white structure that he stopped and dismounted. Only then did our eyes connect, and everything freeze—the noise dropping to a low, barely discernable rumble.

"Will," he said, placing the animal's reins in the hands of an unsuspecting fan who would no doubt be surprised when normal time resumed.

"Palm Sunday?" I said, barely cordial.

"That's what they're calling it?"

I answered by motioning to the palm branches. "They seem pretty excited."

He nodded and looked out over the crowd. "They recognize the prophecy."

"Prophecy?"

"From five hundred years ago. '*Shout, Daughter Jerusalem! See, your king comes to you, righteous and victorious, lowly and riding on a donkey.*'"

"Seems pretty clear," I said.

"But they still don't understand."

I ventured, "Because they want a political king?"

He nodded. Then sadly, he added, "Soon all this excitement will be turned to destroy me."

Despite my own issues, I shook my head. "If they only knew."

He turned to me. "You don't see the similarities?"

"Similarities?"

"In what we're both experiencing." I frowned, and he continued. "Friends misunderstanding us? Abandonment? No one to turn to?"

The realization took hold. Was it possible? Was I, in my own clumsy way, experiencing the slightest whiff of what he was about to undergo? When I turned back to him, he read my thoughts and was already nodding.

"How," I cleared my throat, "how will you endure it?"

"Unlike you, my identity isn't wrapped up in what people think."

"Unlike me?"

"You've been on a rollercoaster, Will. All of your life. Up and down. If you feel loved, you feel worthy. If you feel hated, as you are now, you feel worthless. Up and down. Up and down."

"Everyone wants to be loved."

"But you are. You know that. More than you can imagine. You don't need the fickleness of people to prove it." I glanced down and he continued more gently. "Ever since you were a child you've been on that ride."

"Except this time it feels like I've been thrown off."

"And it's only going to get worse."

I looked to him in concern.

"Remember? I told you from the beginning you'd be tested."

"Yes, but—how can things get worse?"

"Your enemy, the devil, wants to destroy you."

"Well, it looks like he'll have to take a number." I scowled then said, "Aren't you supposed to protect me from this sort of stuff?"

"Or use it."

"Use it?"

He nodded.

"And you call that love?"

"I call it, *setting you free.* You've been bound for decades, a slave to what other people think."

"That's not true."

"It isn't?"

"Okay, it's what Cindy always accused me of, but people aren't that big of a deal to me. That's why I enjoy being alone."

"You enjoy being alone because you're afraid."

"I am not afraid," I argued. "People—they just exhaust me."

"Because you spend all that energy trying to impress them, worrying what they think." He paused, then continued. "We've talked about you being my bride, right? Experiencing my intimacy?"

I nodded, though it was never a metaphor I was comfortable with.

"Well, sadly, for you and me, other people are also in our bed."

I shifted uneasily, his point becoming clear. "And you," I coughed, "you can fix that?"

"Do you remember the book of Job?"

"In part."

He closed his eyes and quoted, *"There is no one on earth like him; he is blameless and upright, a man who fears God and shuns evil."*

"Quite a claim."

"Quite a man. But he was still a slave. He lived in fear that he loved some things on earth more than he loved us."

"And?"

"We let the enemy prove it wasn't true."

"If I recall, you let the devil destroy everything he had."

"Exactly."

I frowned.

Again, he quoted, *"What I feared has come upon me; what I dreaded has happened to me."*

I wasn't sure I liked where this was going. "And—"

"He was freed. Delivered from that fear. Completely."

"A little harsh, wouldn't you say?"

"It had such a strong hold on him, it was the only way. And he pulled through. Even when his wife tried to convince him to curse us, he refused. And when all was said and done, he was not only set free, but rewarded with twice as many of the very things that once imprisoned him. Only now he owned them, instead of them owning him." I looked at him and he shrugged. "We won't be outgiven."

"So . . ." I said, piecing it together, "my reputation, what others think about me—"

"Is your prison."

"And you're going to break me out?"

"Remember what I said in the synagogue? *'I've come to set the captives free?'* With your permission, we'll free you from being enslaved by the judgment of others.

"With the endgame being . . ."

"To see yourself as you really are—as *we* see you; as our Father's favorite son, my favorite brother, and a dear, dear friend." With both a sigh and sad twinkle, he added, "Who I'm so crazy in love with, I'm about to die for."

Memories of his bloody death flickered through my mind. I looked back to the crowd, my eyes beginning to burn. But even as I stood, remembering, and watching the crowd, I realized he completely side-stepped my concern for Sean. "Wait a minute," I said. "You're avoiding the real issue."

With that sad smile of his, he answered, "No, my friend, I'm meeting the real issue head-on." And, just as suddenly as I appeared in the crowd, I was back in my car, pulling up to the south entrance of the school—the fog thicker than ever.

CHAPTER
TWENTY-TWO

THE CAMPUS LAY in eerie silence, fog absorbing nearly every sound. Buildings, not a hundred feet away, dissolved into gray mist. The two students I passed, each holding a Starbucks that had not kicked in, didn't bother to look up, trudging forward in their own version of *The Walking Dead*.

My lecture hall was equally silent. As semesters stretch into weeks then months, classes thin; not because students drop out, but because they've learned how to play me—to put in just enough effort to get a decent grade and beat the system—a skill which, come to think of it, may be the most important thing people glean from higher education.

Down at the lectern I busied myself with papers, discretely counting how many students entered. Not a difficult task since there was only one. Elisha Schwartz, a diehard *Lord of the Rings* fan who changed the color of her hair every few weeks and lived in her own private shire. She was the student you tried never to call upon, and when you did, you hoped she remembered her meds. I stalled an extra minute or two should there be any stragglers. There were none. And when I looked up to begin, it was just in time to catch Elisha finishing reading a text.

"Uh, Dr. Thomas?" she asked.

"Yes, Elisha?"

"There's a, an emergency and I need to leave, like right now, okay?"

"An emergency?"

"Yeah." She stuffed her journal into her backpack, eyes floating in every direction but to me. "And I should leave now 'cause you know how emergencies can be sometimes really not good, so I should really leave. Now." As so often with millennials, her final sentence rose at the end, making it more question than statement. "So, uh, I've got to go?"

"Of course," I said. I watched as she rose and headed toward the door. "Is there anything I can do to help?" I asked.

"No, I think, no thanks. I don't think, thank you."

She left and the room fell back into silence, highlighted only by the soft whir of the heating ducts. I waited a few more minutes before packing up and heading to my office. I thought of stopping by Patricia's but doubted she'd be on campus yet—probably running some trail to burn off that sliver of cake she binged on at yesterday's shower.

Five minutes later, I was shaking the rain off my coat and entering my office. It was a small, cubbyhole of a thing—more walk-in closet than office—with just enough room for a desk and chair, bookshelf, and one extra chair for students pleading to have their grade raised. It smelled of dust, floor wax, and old books from several of my best friends— Frost, Whitman, Dickinson, and dozens of lesser-knowns. I dropped my backpack in the corner (briefcases went out with Dockers) and was startled when my office phone rang. It never rings. After some serious search and rescue, I found it buried under a pile of last semester's papers.

"Hello?"

"Professor Thomas?"

"Yes."

"This is Mary Lambert from Dr. DeVoss's office." (Dr. DeVoss as in Dr. Robert L. DeVoss, as in Vice Chancellor of the University.)

"Yes, uh, how can I help you?"

"Dr. DeVoss was wondering if you could swing by his office for a little chat."

My gut tightened. "Certainly." I fumbled for a pencil and unused scrap of paper. "When would that be?"

"He'd like to meet with you now."

"Now?"

"Yes, do you think that's possible?"

"Well, I—"

"He said the sooner the better."

I like Dr. DeVoss. Despite the fact he was administration, he was a reasonable man. Granted, after the New Year's debacle at my house, he agreed I should be censured, even placed on probation. But given the circumstances, who could blame him? How do you overlook one of your faculty members attacking a kid in front of students at an unsanctioned party—and getting hospitalized in the process?

As a seasoned pro, DeVoss guided the college through good times and bad times, not the least being the whole COVID thing. He's jovial, in his late sixties, with perhaps a bit too much cream filling around the edges, and always wearing a smile. Except this morning when I arrived in his office.

"Please," he motioned to one of two chairs before his desk. "Sit." As I did, he wasted no time cutting to the chase. "You've no doubt seen the news."

"Yes, and I can explain."

"I would be disappointed if you couldn't. But no one is looking for an explanation."

I nodded. "Because they need a scapegoat for past injustices. I get it. But Sean is not that guy. Neither am I."

"You were doing a pretty good imitation of it last night."

"He's innocent."

"May be. However, he's not the purpose of this conversation."

I felt my face growing hot. "My words were taken out of context."

"Nevertheless, they were spoken—before God, the world, and more importantly, two local news crews capturing your visit with the very man charged for sexually assaulting one of our students."

"Charged," I said, "not convicted."

"At the moment, when it comes to the public, there's little difference." He looked down at his carefully organized desk. "Your decision to visit him exhibits some very poor judgment."

"He's my friend."

"And this is your school." He looked back up, holding my gaze. "Dr. Sean Fulton has brought us to the brink of a catastrophe. And you, regardless of your intentions, may have pushed us over the edge. Currently, we're in free fall. And to be frank, I'm not exactly sure how to pull us out."

He was right, of course. And I knew we were well beyond any mea culpa I could provide. He removed his glasses, pressing his eyes shut with thumb and forefinger. I waited. He began slowly rocking in his chair.

"So," I finally asked, "now what?"

Eyes still closed and still rocking, he answered, "Technically, you've broken no morality clause. You're too good of a teacher to fire for being stupid—though, in your case, it seems to be a reoccurring pattern. And, of course, there's the whole tenure issue."

I nodded, waiting.

"However." He stopped rocking and looked at me. "Because of your close involvement with Dr. Fulton and last night's inappropriate comments, I am—until things settle down—putting you on leave of absence."

"Leave of absence?"

"As much for the university as for your own safety."

"My safety?" He gave no answer. "For how long?" I asked.

"I have no idea."

I sat there, mind racing. "By announcing this," I said, "won't you be putting me in the same category as Sean?"

He sighed heavily in agreement. "And without a trial to clear your name."

"Is that fair?"

He shook his head. "No, no, it isn't. But you should have considered that before visiting him and holding your impromptu press conference."

"Which was taken out of context."

He nodded with another sigh. "I'm sure it was."

"What about my students? We just can't cut them off mid-semester."

"I'll speak with your TAs. If necessary, Hendrix can fill in."

I cringed. Morton Hendrix had the unique gift of turning any subject into a cure for insomnia.

We sat another moment before his phone rang.

"Excuse me." He reached for the receiver to answer, "Yes?"

Behind him, I watched trickles of rain slowly snake their way down the window.

"Just now?" He sounded alarmed. "No, no, I'll take care of it." Without further word, he hung up. Once again he pinched his eyes and began to rock, more vigorously than before.

"Is everything all right?" I asked.

He looked up, surprised I was still in the room, and stopped rocking. "I'd like you to clear out your desk," he said. "Immediately."

"Now?"

"As of this moment you're on suspension. We'll call when it's appropriate for you to return to campus." He reached to his desk and straightened some already straightened papers. "If it's appropriate."

"*If?*"

He rose from his chair, preparing to leave the office. "Two alumni have just come forward accusing Sean Fulton of sexual assault."

TWENTY-THREE

WITH HEAD SPINNING, I'd barely passed DeVoss's secretary, who suddenly busied herself typing, before I was in the hall and on the phone. He was right, I was a fool. Not because I spoke up, well maybe that, too, but because I was set up. The call immediately kicked into Sean's voice mail. He was still mad or sleeping it off or both. Who knew? Who cared? All I knew was I wanted to get into his face. Fortunately, I still had enough functioning brain cells to forgo another visit.

Was he innocent? Even big-hearted, village-idiot me had my doubts. And if he was, he could have at least warned me others might come forward. I reached the end of the hall, threw open the door, and stepped into a heavier rain than before. I called him again. Same results. If he thought he could put me off that easily, not a chance. I tried again as I continued down the sidewalk, head bent against the weather. Then again. The campus was filling with students and I caught more than one staring at me—apparently surprised I showed up. But I said nothing. What could I say? Things were too knotted to untangle—and tightening by the minute. Darlene hated me. Amber hated me. For all intents and purposes, my job was history. Oh, and the entire world knew I'd sided with a possible rapist. Not only sided, but actually blamed his victim!

"Things aren't always as they appear," I'd said. Apparently I was more right than I knew.

I dialed Belinda. Another no answer.

A clump of students who had gathered under an awning ceased talking as I approached. I stared at the ground and kept walking.

There had to be something I could do, some course of action. But, try as I might, nothing came to mind. I was trapped with no place to turn. And Yeshua? True to form, he was nowhere to be seen. "*A loving Father*," he'd said. Really? What loving father would put a son through something like this? But I'd been warned, he said. *Warned?* More like played. Just as badly as I'd been played by Sean. "*I promise you things would get tough,*" he'd said. Well, that was one promise he did manage to keep. "*And with your permission—*" *My* permission! Seriously? As if I have a choice. And if I did, then take my name off the list, because no one should have to go through something like this.

Instantly, the day became night. No light, except a full moon shining through a wispy layer of clouds. And no rain. The sidewalk had turned to dirt and twigs crunching under my feet. I slowed, squinting into the darkness. The best I could see, I was in a grove of trees.

"No!" I exclaimed, "I'm not in the mood!"

But the vision continued.

"I said I'm not in the—"

I stopped. Ten yards ahead, in the mottled light and shadow, I caught a glimpse of pale clothing. I eased closer. Men. Some propped against the base of the trees, while others stretched out on the ground. No one moved or talked. Not a sound except the quiet stirring of overhead leaves and what sounded like muffled snores.

Then I heard it. A faint cry in the distance off to my right. I turned, peering into the shadows. There it was again. A choked gasp. Keeping half an eye on the men, I moved to investigate. I passed one tree after another until I heard it again. Much closer. And as I rounded the final tree, I saw him—sprawled out face down on the ground. Gasping in uneven breaths. His hands stretched before him, clawing at the dirt with clenched fists.

"Father—"

I froze, stunned.

He lifted his face. In the moonlight it glistened with sweat. I watched as he struggled to rise to his hands and knees. An unearthly moan rose from deep inside him, turning to a cry he managed to swallow. Now, on all fours, he shook his head back and forth like a wounded animal while gasping, "Father—Father . . ."

I wanted to help—to run to his side. But I sensed the moment was too sacred, too holy to interrupt.

He reached a trembling hand to the tree beside him, fighting to stand, then slipped, falling back to the ground. He tried again, using both hands, groping his way up the trunk until he stood swaying, knees barely holding. Once again, he raised a face soaked in sweat and tears. And something else. Dark in the light, almost black. Blood. Beads of blood had appeared on his forehead, his cheeks. I stopped breathing and could only stare. I read of this happening to men in combat. Soldiers under such impossible stress their blood pressure rose until it burst the tiny capillaries in their face.

He was literally sweating blood.

He took another breath, chest heaving. "No!" He pushed away from the tree, staggering like a drunk, pacing like a caged animal. "No! Take this cup from me!"

My throat knotted; my vision blurred with tears. He'd had enough. He could go no further. God's claim that he wants to make us, "*whole and complete, lacking in nothing*?" Not true. How could it be with such suffering? Yeshua's and, to a much lesser degree, my own.

"*Free will,*" he had said. "*Our greatest gift from the Father.*" And, as I watched, I saw it in action. Here, before me, his very son living it out. Unable to endure any more, he was calling it quits. He stumbled, nearly caught his balance before falling back to the ground. He was shaking now, trembling at the horror before him. A horror he chose to escape.

Until . . .

His body stiffened. He sucked in a ragged breath, then another. Mustering the last of his strength, he shouted, "No!" But it was a different no. Once again, he rose onto his hands and knees, the tortured man/animal. Once again he lifted his face, covered in sweat and tears and blood. But there was a different look in his eyes. Gasping, fighting to breathe, he choked out the words: "No! Not my will—yours!"

"Are you all right?"

I looked up to see a pair of shaggy-haired students hovering over me—one sporting a moth-eaten beard. I was hunched over, leaning against the back of a bench along the sidewalk.

"Yeah," I said, taking an uneven breath and straightening up.

"You sure?"

I nodded, wiped the rain and tears from my face.

"Too bad," the bearded one said.

I looked at him quizzically.

"We were hoping for a heart attack."

Before I could respond, they turned and continued down the walk through the rain.

I kept a hand on the bench to steady myself. The vision had been short. Yeshua hadn't said a word, at least to me. But he'd said plenty. Still, those brief moments did not lessen the betrayal I felt. Or the abandonment. And yet, to witness him enduring his own crucible—and to successfully pass, gave me a type of—comfort. Assurance. I wasn't alone. Someone had been through it before me. Only worse. And succeeded. And it was that knowledge that somehow, someway, gave me enough strength to carry on—or at least try.

But try what? I looked across campus. What was my next move? Clean out my desk and run with my tail between my legs? No. There had to be something I could do, someone I could talk— Of course. Patricia Swenson. If she didn't understand the details, and I didn't expect her to, she could at least pray with me. Well, not *with*, I still hadn't developed the knack of praying out loud, but she could pray for me. I turned from the bench, bumping into a couple co-eds, who had no trouble recognizing me or hiding the disgust on their faces, and headed for Patricia's office.

ᔕ

The Health Science department was new—mostly glass and steel with exposed aluminum air ducts. Her office was on the second floor. I wasn't surprised at seeing an immaculate desk and books on dustless, plexiglass shelves, arranged by size, not author. She wore glasses and was grading papers, looking even more lovely than I remembered. She glanced up, startled to see me in the doorway.

"Will." She removed her glasses. "What are you doing here?"

"I wanted to explain."

"Explain?"

I stepped inside. "You've seen the reports?"

"On the news, yes, of course. You've become quite the celebrity." Her demeanor from that first day at Bible Club returned. Pleasant but brittle.

"It isn't true, you know."

"And what part is that?"

"What part?" I said, "None of it."

"None of—"

"Some of it, yes, well maybe, but not the news report."

"What you said wasn't true?"

"Right," I said. "I mean, no. It was taken out of context." I looked to the empty chair in front of her desk. She followed my gaze but made no offer.

"So," she continued, "when you visited Dr. Fulton and told the world the girl was to blame, you really didn't mean the girl was to blame?"

"No, that's not what I said."

"Hmm—" She slipped her glasses back on as if to return to her papers.

"Patricia—"

She glanced back up. Her expression suddenly changed, seeing someone behind me. "Oh, hello, Ashley."

I turned to see one of the Bible Club students standing in the doorway, her eyes darting between Patricia and myself. "I, uh," she cleared her throat. "I can come back later."

"Hi," I said.

She ignored me and looked back to Patricia.

"Is it 9:30 already?" Patricia asked, glancing at her watch.

"We can meet another time if it's more convenient," Ashley said.

"No, now is good." Patricia looked at me and continued, "Dr. Thomas was just leaving."

"I—" My mouth was dry. "I can wait. How long will you two be?"

Patricia gave a smile that didn't quite make it to her eyes. "I'm afraid I have a class immediately afterward."

"And—after that?" I asked.

"Actually, today is not a good day. In fact, the rest of my week is booked."

"It will only take a few minutes," I said. "I just need to explain—"

"Seriously, Doctor," she interrupted. "Our discussion needs to be some other time."

I stood a moment, unsure what to do. I looked to the girl who kept her eyes locked on Patricia. Then to Patricia who kept her gaze on me.

"Well, alright then." I coughed slightly. "Some other time, then."

"That would be best."

I nodded, then turned and headed down the hall—my abandonment complete.

CHAPTER
TWENTY-FOUR

THE RAIN FELL harder as I passed students rushing for the safety of buildings. The few who looked up recognized me. I fought the impulse to drop my eyes. Not in pride—what pride could I possibly have left—but in determination. I would get through this. I was not alone. He had faced it before me. My betrayal and abandonment didn't hold a candle to his, but I suppose that was the point. If he'd been through this, and so much more, I at least had someone who understood.

In the distance I heard voices. Another vision? I wasn't sure, but the other students seemed to hear it as well. A group meeting in this weather? Whatever was happening, I figured it best to avoid any type of gathering, so I took the long way around to my office.

When I arrived, I was surprised to see Bertrand, head of campus security, standing outside my door. He was big, black, and 270 if a pound. A former Marine, if I recall. We exchanged occasional greetings over the years.

"Dr. Thomas."

I shook my head. "Don't waste any time, do they?"

He didn't smile but gave the slightest nod for what I took to be understanding.

"I'll just grab the essentials," I said, pulling out my keys and unlocking the door, "to tide me over 'til I come back."

He gave another nod, then quietly added, "The sooner, the better."

I turned to him. "How's that?"

He stepped back from the door. "I'll wait out here 'til you're ready."

I frowned at the haste as I entered my office. I grabbed my backpack and began stuffing it with far too many books, friends to pull me through, the more the merrier. I also tossed in a stack of papers to grade, and framed photos of Amber, Siggy and, yes, even Cindy. (Call me an optimist.)

I slung the pack over my shoulder and staggered a little under its weight. I took one last look around the room. For years this had been my second home, spending as much time here as on the island. Finally, with a deep breath, I turned, stepped into the hallway, and shut the door.

I'd barely finished locking it when I saw Bertrand's outstretched palm. I fumbled to pull the key off the key-ring and was surprised at how my fingers trembled. I held it out, staring as his meaty hand wrap around it.

Then, without a word, he turned and we began the long walk down the hall. The walls were covered with photographs of esteemed faculty members, many I knew personally, along with dozens of commemorative plaques and department awards, a couple even for me. The backpack dug into my shoulder and I slipped my other arm into the other strap to distribute the weight. When we arrived at the double glass doors, Bertrand pushed one open and motioned for me to pass.

The rain had let up some, but the din of the distant crowd had grown louder—punctuated by an indistinguishable voice on a bullhorn. It seemed to come from the quad, one set of buildings over. The same quad we would have to cross to reach my car.

Before we started down the steps, Bertrand pulled up the hood of his camo raincoat and turned to me. "You ready for this?"

I motioned to the sound. "It's about Sean? Dr. Fulton?"

"Stay close."

He barely spoke the words before the rain stopped. Instantly. I now stood in bright, hot sunlight. Below me stretched a large courtyard where an angry mob with raised fists was shouting—peasants I'd seen that first Palm Sunday. I turned to Bertrand, but he had disappeared. And when I looked for Yeshua, he was nowhere to be found. The scene flickered and I was back on the department's steps with Bertrand. I adjusted my backpack, gave him a nod, and we started down to the sidewalk.

As we moved along the buildings, the bullhorn grew louder, clearer. It was a young man's voice, trying to start a chant. "What do we want?" he shouted. When there was no response, he answered, "Justice!" Again, he shouted, "What do we want?"

A smattering of voices replied, "Justice."

"When do we want it?"

More joined in. "Now!"

"What do we want?" he repeated.

"Justice!"

"When do we want it?"

The voices grew louder, angrier. "Now!"

We rounded the final building and there they were—sixty or so students standing in the rain. On a bench in the center, shouting into the bullhorn, stood the student from my British Lit class, Lucas Harrington. "What do we want?"

"Justice!" they shouted.

"When do we want it?"

"Now!"

As I approached the crowd, he caught sight of me and hesitated. The students turned, following his gaze. Unable to help myself, I slowed.

"Let's go, Doctor." Bertrand's big hand pressed against the small of my back. There was another flicker, and I returned to the hot sun, this time walking down a narrow, stone-paved street, my backpack far heavier than I remembered. Surrounding me, on all sides, were the same shouting and jeering peasants I'd seen moments earlier. I turned, searching the crowd, but there was still no sign of Yeshua.

Then I was back in the quad, the backpack digging into my shoulders, growing heavier with every step. I adjusted it as we moved deeper into the crowd. In marked contrast to the shouting on the sun-scorched street, these students in the rain had gone quiet, stepping aside to let us pass. I threw a look over to Lucas, who had lowered his bullhorn, watching with the others. But the silence lasted only a moment. Soon, a stirring began. Murmurs rippled through the crowd.

I was back on the street, surrounded by the shouting and jeers. Then back on campus. Then the street. And still no sign of Yeshua. Only then did the realization sink in. The mob of peasants was not looking at someone else. They were looking at me. They were glaring and shouting at me! The weight on my shoulders grew impossibly heavy, and I staggered forward, nearly falling. When I looked up, a co-ed stepped in front of me, her hair wet and stringy from the rain, defiantly blocking my path until she saw Bertrand's look and pulled back.

"Go home!" another student shouted.

Some cheered in agreement.

"We don't want you here!"

More cheers.

Back in the blistering sun, I stumbled again, this time falling under the crushing weight on my back.

"You're pathetic!" a male student shouted.

I looked up to the taunting, screaming faces of the street, then struggled to stand, using all my strength to rise on trembling legs.

"Shame on you!" another co-ed yelled in my face.

Everything morphed—faces from the present blending with the past—students, peasants, all filled with rage. Hot liquid splashed into my face. Coffee thrown by a student. A peasant spitting on me, his saliva mixing with the rain and coffee stung my eyes. Someone lunged from the crowd, striking me so hard stars danced in my vision as a Roman guard beat him back. "You're sick!" a student shouted. More coffee, along with the hard edge of a cup, or stone.

"Hang in there, Doc," Bertrand shouted, his arm guiding me along.

"What do we want?" The chant resumed.

"Justice!"

"When do we want it?"

"Oh, Doctor . . ." I turned to see Gretchen in her wheelchair, eyes filled with sorrow and disappointment.

"Now!"

"What do we want?"

"Justice!"

How long this continued, I can't be certain. But as we approached the end of the quad, the first-century faces appeared less and less frequently until they were replaced by the remaining students along the crowd's edge.

We continued forward; only a few, all male, followed us into the parking lot.

"Nice paint job, Thomas," someone shouted.

I looked to my car. Even through the rain I could see it had been keyed, bumper to bumper.

"You doin' okay?" Bertrand asked.

I nodded but couldn't answer.

One of the students shouted, "Cool!"

I turned to see him looking up from his phone. "They just found him!" he yelled.

I scowled, making it clear I didn't understand.

"Your buddy, the rapist!" he shouted. "He hung himself."

CHAPTER
TWENTY-FIVE

I OPENED THE car door and, with Bertrand's help, fell into the seat.

"You sure you're alright?" he asked.

I may have nodded, I don't remember. I do remember my hands shaking so violently I could barely get the key into the ignition.

But the nightmare wasn't over.

I'd just got onto the freeway, when Amber called. With one hand on the wheel, I dug into my pocket and pulled out the phone.

"Hey," I croaked. There was no response. "Amber?"

"I broke Mom's car!" she sobbed.

"What?"

"Don't be mad." She sniffed, regaining her composure, and explained. "Darlene, she said she wouldn't take me driving. She could have missed the stupid ferry and took the next one, but—" another sniff, "she wouldn't, so I did it myself."

"Did it— You went driving on your own?"

"Don't be mad."

I shifted the phone to my other hand. "Where are you?"

"I hit a tree."

"You hit—"

"I swerved to miss something, a branch or something, and I kinda went off the road."

"You—"

"Instead of the brake, I hit the stupid gas pedal and—don't be mad!"

"I'm not mad," I said, trying to sound calm. "Are you okay?"

"I kept going 'cause I thought I was hitting the brake and—"

"Are you alright?'

"Yes, no. I mean, I'm stuck cause it's all smushed in around me."

"The car?"

She began crying again. "I'm really sorry."

"But you're okay?"

"I just told you."

"Where are you?"

"I don't know. It's all rainy and there's nothing but trees. I got pretty far, 'til I got stuck."

"Alright, it's alright," I said, as much for her as for myself. "As long as you're okay. Did you call 911?"

"Don't be stupid."

"I'm sorry?"

"I can't have my baby in jail!"

"They're not going to—"

She suddenly screamed in pain.

"Are you alright? What's wrong?"

"The baby, he's— oh, crap, my jeans are all wet. He broke my water!" She screamed again.

"Amber?"

"It hurts!"

"Amber, where are you?"

"I told you," she gasped, "I don't know!"

"Call 911. You need help. Call them. Now!"

"No! I—" She swallowed back another scream and dropped the phone.

"Amber! Amber, can you hear me?"

Nothing but panting gasps.

"Amber, can you hear me?"

Another cry—muffled and eerie.

"Amber!"

When it was clear she wouldn't or couldn't answer, I tried putting her on hold (which meant accidentally disconnecting her) and called 911. I glanced at my watch, grateful that if I hurried, I could catch the next ferry back to the island. I pulled into the fast lane. Once the dispatcher picked up and I, "explained the nature of my emergency," she hesitated, unsure what to do. Finally, she patched me over to the sheriff's department on the island, which proved equally unhelpful.

"And you don't know what road she's on?" the deputy asked.

"I told you, she's not on a road; she drove off it."

"And what road was that?"

"I don't know! She doesn't know. And she can't see it from the car."

"If she doesn't know what road she's on—"

"She's fourteen, she was teaching herself to drive."

An RV pulled directly in front of me. I hit the brakes, blowing my horn—more in frustration at the deputy than the driver.

"Listen," I said, "I live at 1420 Pinehurst; she can't be far from there."

"We'll send a car out to your home."

"She won't be at my home."

"Sir, we have to start somewhere." My phone beeped and I looked to see it was Darlene calling. "Can you hang on a moment?" I asked. Before the deputy could respond, I pressed what I hoped to be the incoming button and answered, "Darlene?"

"I just got off the phone with Amber," she said. "Why did you hang up on her?"

"I—"

"I'm still on the island, at the ferry terminal. I'm turning around to find her. When can you get here?"

"I'll be able to catch the next one out."

"Well—hurry!"

I was first on the ferry heading back to the island. I didn't bother to get out of the car because the storm had grown worse—both on the water and in my head. Sean Fulton gone? How was that possible? What was he thinking? Had he become so drunk he didn't realize what he was doing? And when did he do it? Last night after our fight? This morning after the two alumni came forward? The questions roiled in my head. Along with another—was his action an admission of guilt, or did the pressure push him over the edge? Of course, everyone would conclude it was guilt. But they didn't know Sean. How he used that charming, dressed-to-the-T exterior to protect his vulnerable, artsy side.

No, they didn't know him like I knew him. Or maybe, after all these years, I was the one who didn't know.

I sat in the car taking one deep breath after another as the ferry lumbered and shuttered its way through the storm. What's going on? I prayed, I raged and, yes, threw out a few oaths along the way. After all, hadn't he said he'd rather me be mad at him than to cut off communication? Well, I was doing my part.

"Why?" I shouted at the roof of the car. "What are you trying to prove? You say you're a God of love! This isn't love!" No response. "Talk to me! Give me a straight answer for once! Can you at least do that?"

But of course, he didn't. Or maybe he couldn't. Maybe I was screaming too loud to hear that, "*still, small voice.*"

But how could I not scream? Everything was destroyed—my friend, my career, my reputation. And now this emergency with Amber. The ferry swayed, rolling harder from the wind and waves. *"Master, don't you care that we're about to drown?"*

That first day, on that cliff in Nazareth, he promised things would be hard—that he'd take the words of the Bible and make them flesh and blood. "*Incarnate,*" he said. In me. "*So, we can rule together,*" he said. Absurd. Impossible. Yet those were his words, not mine. "*Come down out of the stands and play.*" I did! Maybe not as well as I'd like, but I played. Hadn't I just proven it on the campus walking through my own Gethsemane? I obeyed. I'd said yes. It had killed me, stripping away everything, *everything* I held dear. But I obeyed!

Obeyed, but apparently not died. Not yet.

Head throbbing, I laid it on the steering wheel and wept. "Please, God—" Because I remembered, all too well, Christ's reward for his obedience in the Garden. "Please. Not Amber."

CHAPTER
TWENTY-SIX

RIVULETS OF RAIN ran off the yellow, foul-weather gear of the crewmen as he unlatched the safety chains at the front of the ferry. He'd not even dragged them aside, before I gunned the car and shot past him and up the ramp—as he shouted things I'm glad I couldn't hear. I passed the terminal gate and approached the intersection at the top of the hill when Darlene called.

"I found her!" she said, out of breath.

"Where?"

Over rustling brush and noise, I heard, "McElroy Road. A couple miles from the shopping center."

"Is she—what's that sound?"

"Car horn. She's honking the horn to be found. Smart kid."

I cranked the wheel hard to the right and slid through the intersection. "I'm ten minutes away."

Four minutes later, I arrived. Spotting Darlene's car, I parked behind it, threw open my door, and ran across the road. I followed the mud and trampled grass all the way into a stand of cedars where I spotted the car. Amber had done some fancy driving, managing to dodge the trees for a good twenty yards before they stopped her. The driver's side appeared crushed against a large cedar. The passenger side was equally destroyed by an earlier hit. As I approached, Darlene was bent down at what was left of the driver's window.

"Hey!" I shouted over the rain.

She looked up then leaned back down to Amber, saying something I couldn't hear.

"How's she doing?" I yelled.

"Uncle Will!" Even with the rain and her muffled voice, I heard the terror.

"You call the sheriff?" I shouted.

"They just left your house!" Darlene yelled.

"That's thirty minutes away!"

"Uncle Will!"

The closer I came, the more damage I saw. The front hood was crumpled with the engine shoved toward the driver's compartment by one large and very stubborn stump. It was a wonder Amber survived.

Covering my concern, I shouted, "You do thorough work." Then as I arrived, to lighten the mood, I added, "You know this is coming out of your allow—" I stopped. Through the shattered window I saw she was completely pinned—in front, by the dash and steering wheel, to her left by the crushed driver's door, and to her right by the console.

"Uncle Will . . ."

"It's okay, kiddo. The sheriff will get you out of there and—"

"I'm having my baby!"

"Right, and we'll get you to the—"

"I'm having him now!" She barely finished the words before her face twisted. She gulped back a scream, but only for a moment before it exploded from somewhere deep within her.

I turned to Darlene who lowered her voice. "Look at her legs."

I looked back through the broken glass. Amber's legs were shoved tightly against each other with no room to move. I turned to Darlene. She nodded, pale and grave. If Amber couldn't separate her legs, how could she give birth?

I spun back to the car and yanked at the door.

"Will—"

With adrenaline surging, I pulled again, then again. It didn't budge. Getting to her from this side was impossible. I raced to the other.

"I already tried," Darlene called as I arrived at the passenger door. "It's jammed too."

I pulled at it over and over. She was right, and I slammed the door in frustration.

I could feel Amber watching, her eyes pleading.

Blood roared in my ears as I searched for a solution. There was a small opening between the passenger door and center post. I grabbed hold and pulled. The door gave slightly, but not enough. I took a better hold and tried again, yanking, jerking. The metal dug into my hands until they bled but I felt no pain. And I saw no movement.

"Uncle Will . . ."

"Hang on!" I turned and searched behind me—looking for a rock, a limb, something. I spotted a fallen branch several yards away and raced to pick it up. It was large and unwieldy but would have to do. I ran back to the car and worked the end into the opening. Once I succeeded, I used the center post to leverage the limb against the door and pushed, throwing all my weight behind it—until the limb snapped in two.

Amber screamed in pain; I guessed another contraction.

I stepped back, holding the limb. There had to be some way in. I knew cars. My drunk of a father made sure of it—humiliating and taunting me the entire summer we tore one apart and put it back together. But this?

"Will?"

I looked across the roof to Darlene who was hoping for some answer. I shook my head. I had nothing except a terrified niece who could very well lose her baby—or worse.

"Yeshua—" I whispered. Please . . ."

As usual, there was no response. No visions. No burning bush. Just an unborn baby about to die, a car impossible to open, and a wooden branch serving as a sorry tool against the sheet metal. Wait! A tool! That's what I needed. A *real* tool!

I dropped the limb and ran back toward my car.

"Will!" Darlene shouted. "Where are you going?"

"Shopping center!" I yelled. "The hardware store!"

"Well . . . Hurry!"

∾

I raced down the store's aisle, fumbling to hold all the items—crowbar, sledgehammer, assorted wrenches, screwdrivers. Up front, the cashier, a ruddy-faced kid in the throes of puberty, was ringing up miscellaneous car parts for a father and his young boy—air filter, belts, various what-nots.

Deciding to forgo the formalities, I rushed past them and headed for the door.

"Hey!" the cashier shouted. Then, invoking the full authority of his red vest and name tag, he repeated. "Hey!"

"I'll be back," I yelled as the doors whisked open and I ran into the parking lot. I'd barely reached the car—not before dropping the ratchet set, scooping it back up, while dropping a pair of pliers—when a potential linebacker, in similar red vest and name tag, ran out of the store shouting, "What are you doing? Get back here!"

I threw the tools into the front seat and jumped inside, barely having time to lock the doors before he arrived.

He pounded on the glass and yelled, "I'll call the police!"

"Yes! Please!" I said, starting the car. "We're two miles up the road!"

"What are you doing with all that stuff?"

I dropped the car into gear and raced off. "Delivering a baby!"

CHAPTER
TWENTY-SEVEN

I RETURNED TO the wrecked car—my arms, hands, and pockets loaded with tools. Darlene was on the phone while Amber was trying to breathe through her pain. The poor girl's face was drenched in sweat, hair in wet strings. When she saw the tools, her eyes widened.

"It's okay," I shouted through the window. "I've got a plan!"

Seeing the crowbar, she cried out, "Aunt Darlene!"

"It'll help move your legs," I said.

"*Aunt Darlene!*" My explanation was less than helpful.

"You know what you're doing with all that stuff?" Darlene asked.

"Of course. I'm a guy."

She gave me a dubious look, then returned to her phone call, saying, "It's Will."

"Who's that?" I shouted as I headed for the passenger side.

"Patricia."

"Patricia Swenson?"

"*Doctor* Swenson," she said.

Of course. I'd nearly forgotten. I dumped the tools onto the soggy ground next to the door.

"Hurry!" Darlene shouted. "She's pushing!"

"She can't!" I bent down and yelled through the window to Amber. "Not yet. It's too soon!"

She stopped panting just long enough to flash me a homicidal glare.

"That's not how it works, pal," Darlene said.

I looked from Amber to Darlene then back to Amber—once again out of my depth. I grabbed the crowbar and went to work. I wedged it between the center post and door, pushing and prying. It creaked and groaned, slowly giving way.

"Okay, kiddo," Darlene yelled to Amber. "Patricia says it's time to lose the pants."

"I can't!" Amber shouted. "There's no room!"

"You got a little. I see it."

"But—" she threw a furtive look in my direction.

"Now," Darlene demanded. "Do it now!"

I made it clear I was focused on the crowbar and, reluctantly, she unzipped her jeans.

The door separated enough from the post for me to grab the sledgehammer. With eight or nine heavy blows, I enlarged the opening enough to squeeze my body through as jagged metal caught and ripped my pants. With the dashboard and steering wheel trapping her, my best line of attack was the console between us. As Amber squirmed, slipping the jeans over her hips, I used the hammer, pliers, and wrench, but only managed to break off small chunks of it.

"How's it going?" Darlene shouted.

"Not yet!" I yelled.

Amber was sobbing again as she pulled her jeans down her thighs. "Gross—this is so gross."

"Can you turn her," Darlene called, "get her on her side?"

"No. The steering wheel and dash have her pinned."

Amber began another contraction. But this time, she cried out two words. Just two. *"Uncle Will!"* I went cold—paralyzed by responsibility and by the fear of what could happen. Dead baby. Hemorrhaging niece . . .

"Yeshua," I whispered. There was no answer. Except—

His comments on praise bubbled up in my brain. *"Push out your fear with my praise."* Ridiculous! Praise for what? That Amber hadn't been killed? No. You said it yourself—you never play defense. Then praise for what? The disaster in front of me? Forget it! There's nothing here but our stupid mistakes, what you call free will—free will that alienated my niece, free will she drove the car, free will she's pregnant. No. There's nothing to praise here, nothing good. Just . . . you. I swallowed. The only good is you.

I took a deep breath. The Eeyore in me was paralyzed with past failures—and future what-ifs.

But there was Yeshua. His character. His love.

And so, using free will, I took hold of my thoughts and dug in, refusing to look at the situation. Not refusing, really just—replacing. Replacing my thoughts of past failures and future fears with his goodness. With who he is. And, like the balloon he was so fond of, I felt my fear slowly being pushed aside.

But only for a moment until it roared back with a vengeance.

Memories of the same panic I felt minutes earlier when madly racing through the hardware store—the boy and his dad looking up from the check-out counter where they were buying—wait a minute. The boy and his dad. Me. My dad. What would he say? Besides the constant ranting and ridicule? He knew cars. He'd taught me cars. I looked back to Amber—the dash and steering wheel that were impossible to move, the console that would not budge, the seat that—

The seat!

I pulled back out of the car into the rain, grabbed the socket set, and re-entered. With more effort than my ravaged back should allow, I squirmed over the broken console, bending and contorting myself until I reached behind her seat and saw the track and the bolts holding it down.

"He's coming!" Amber yelled.

"Is he crowning?" Darlene shouted.

"What?" Amber cried.

"Put your hand down there," Darlene yelled, "can you feel him?"

Remembering bits and flurries of my dad's instruction, I began unbolting the track, using the hammer to— *"don't ruin the threads, you moron, just loosen them."*

"No way!" Amber screamed.

"What's wrong?" Darlene shouted.

"He can't fit!"

"Trust me, he'll fit."

"What's that?" Darlene said into the phone. "Hang on, I'll put you on speaker."

Patricia's voice came on, faint but audible through the rain and broken glass. "Hi, Ambrosia."

"I can't—" Amber panted. "I can't—I quit!"

"Of course you can, sweetheart," Patricia's voice remained calm and assuring. "Just let your body take over."

"I can't!"

"Your body can."

"You can do this," Darlene encouraged.

The three of them continued talking up front, while I continued working in back. The wrench slipped more than once, taking sizeable chunks out of my knuckles, but at last, the bolts gave way. I yanked hard on the seat.

"What are you doing?" Amber cried.

I yanked again. "Push," I called.

"I am pushing!"

"No, the seat. Push back on the seat!"

She did, as I continued to yank until, screaming in alarm, she flew back a good fifteen inches, her knees now clear of the steering wheel.

"Atta girl!" Darlene shouted. Then into the phone, "She can move."

But not enough.

"The stupid console," she cried. "It's in the way, I can't get out."

"But you can turn," Darlene shouted. "Right? You can turn on your side?"

I pulled myself back into the front seat as Amber struggled to turn.

"That's it," Darlene yelled, "you're doing great."

Amber locked eyes with me, grimacing in pain but also determination, as she inched her way around until she was facing me—two feet apart.

"Alright!" Darlene shouted.

"Good girl," Patricia repeated.

"He's coming!" Amber screamed, "He's coming!"

"That's great," Patricia said. "Keep pushing."

"I can't!"

"Yes, you can. Your body can do amazing things. Keep pushing."

"I can't!"

Ignoring her, Patricia continued, "Will, are you still in the car?"

"Yes."

"Okay. You need to help her now. I want you to raise her leg. You've got to open the pathway."

"Bend your leg, sweetheart," Darlene said. "To clear the steering wheel."

For the first time I let my eyes drop to Amber's groin—the mucus, the water, the trickling blood. I closed my eyes, fighting the queasiness.

"Will. Will, are you there?"

I opened my eyes. "Yeah, I'm here."

"Lift up her leg and keep it there. And Ambrosia, keep pushing. You can do this, girl."

"I leaned over the console and reached out, keeping my eyes fixed on Amber's as I took her leg and helped raised it.

"He's coming!" Amber screamed, "He's coming!"

"Don't let him fall," Patricia said.

Amber struggled to move. "I can't, I can't reach him."

"Will, don't let him fall."

I reached further over the console, its broken edges digging into my chest—one hand holding her leg, the other stretched below.

Another scream and suddenly I saw him, his head.

The women continued their encouragement. "That's it, Amber. That's it, sweetie, keep him coming, you're doing great—"

A final cry and scream and he was falling—slipping out of her and falling. He landed in my hand—a major league catch, if I do say so—of a strange-looking, alien creature covered in slime.

"You did it!" Darlene shouted. "She did it!"

"Alright," Patricia said. "Now, Will, hand him to her. Get him onto her chest, and Ambrosia, do your best to dry him. Cover him and keep him warm."

I did as I was told, carefully balancing him as I raised the squirming new life to his mother. Tears rolled down Amber's sweaty face as, staring in awe, she took him.

"What about the cord?" I asked.

"Later," Patricia said. "Just get him dry and warm."

I nodded, motioned for Amber to lift her sweatshirt so she could hold him against her. As she did, I looked back to him for one final surprise.

"Uh, guys." I glanced up to the window where Darlene was wiping tears and rain from her face.

"Guys, I'm no doctor but—I think it's a girl."

TWENTY-EIGHT

IN THE TWILIGHT, I rowed out to the center of the channel. The boat quietly cut through water as flat as glass, not a hint of wind. Other than a single gull drifting overhead, the stillness was absolute. The muscles in my shoulders and back still ached, but I told myself it was a necessary ache to stretch out the stiffness from their abuse inside my sister's wrecked car. The silence was good too. And needed. Not that I didn't appreciate Darlene's and Patricia's visit on this, Amber's first day home from the hospital—Amber's and little Billie-Jean's. (Why she chose that name is beyond me; surely she knew Billie was a nickname for William . . . or Will.) In any case, I needed this time to be alone. Just me and—I looked to the cardboard box on the seat before me—Sean.

Minutes after Billie-Jean's birth, both the sheriff and fire department arrived—along with their Jaws of Life, a powerful little contraption accomplishing in seconds what would have taken me hours. From there, they transported them to a hospital on the mainland. There was some tearing, and given the less-than-sterile environment of the delivery room, there was rightful concern of infection.

Of course, their stay meant mine as well—another cheap motel, this one a mere two and a half minutes away. Darlene and Patricia thought I was overprotective, teasing me about being a nervous "new father." And, though I appreciated the two of them resuming communication with me, I ignored their advice to go home.

Just as they ignored my assurance that Amber and I could handle the baby on our own. A fact best illustrated by today's three-car motorcade from the hospital to the ferry, to Billie-Jean's new home. Of course, it didn't stop with that. Once we arrived, the two women flitted and fretted about the house, rearranging every room, especially Amber's, for the baby—(a temporary situation, I was told, until I could be moved to the laundry room so the child would have a decent nursery). Then there was the afternoon trip to the store for formula, diapers, clothes, and the thousand and one things neither Amber nor I had a clue about.

But Amber was a quick study and definitely the teachers' pet. The two women spoke and taught and giggled with her in a language, that once again made it clear I was an outsider. But that was okay. There was plenty for me to do—like feeding and cleaning up after the animals. Siggy had been his usual cooperative self, eating and doing his business outside whenever the neighbor kid remembered to stop by and let him out. Karl, on the other hand, was vintage Karl. In typical feline style, he voiced his protest of being abandoned by refusing to use the cat box. Choosing my bedroom carpet as a substitute, he made it clear who he blamed.

Then there was the weather stripping to replace around the back door. *"That's not a draft, I feel, is it?"* The plugs for the receptacles I should go out and buy. *"You don't want her to be electrocuted, do you?"* And the ancient black spot in the corner of the living room ceiling. *"You sure it's not mold? You know how dangerous mold can be?"* All that to say, I was given plenty of chores to stay out from underfoot. And, yes, I clearly saw the handwriting on the wall—soon to be repainted in pastel-pinks with fluffy-white clouds and an overabundance of butterflies.

But there were the other moments, ones I hadn't known even existed.

We were in Amber's room when they asked me to hold the baby. I was nervous, of course, and more than a little clumsy. But, rest assured, I had plenty of tutors. And there, in my arms, I saw her for the first time; I mean really saw her. So fragile, so helpless—and full of such possibilities. Then there were her features. I've never seen eyelashes so long. Lips so tiny and perfect. And when she yawned— I still can't explain the stirring I felt inside. Cindy and I never got around to having children, but this . . . She wasn't mine, I knew that, and yet this child, this life so new and unspoiled, shared part of my DNA. And as I watched her blink at a world she didn't understand, a beautiful and dangerous place where she would need someone to guide and instruct her, a sobering responsibility rose within me. And honor. And then she smiled. Only for a moment, but a bond was forged for life.

"She likes you," Darlene whispered.

"Just gas," Amber said.

Patricia's response was a bit more insightful. "The perfect Easter gift, wouldn't you say?"

"Easter?" I turned to her in surprise. "That's right," I exclaimed, "today is Easter."

Patricia smiled. "A good time for resurrection."

Darlene nodded. "And new beginnings."

Now, three hours later, as the sun set, Sean and I were in the boat, just the two of us. I quit rowing and pulled up the oars so we could drift in silence—five, ten minutes. Eventually, I turned to the box of ashes. "Why?" I asked. "No note? No attempt to clear your name?" I looked off to the horizon, the smear of pink and violet already starting to fade. "And if you couldn't, if this was some monster inside you couldn't kick, why wouldn't you let me help?"

Of course, there was no answer—just the quiet lap of water.

I reached for the box and pulled off the lid. Another moment passed before I lifted it over the side of the boat and poured out the contents. There was a faint hiss as the ashes hit the water. I knew I should say something.

Something profound, poetic. After all, we were English professors. Instead, I could only say, "Peace, my friend. I hope you've finally found peace."

I sat in the stillness, watching the ashes slowly spread in the water. Oddly, there were no tears. Just a hole inside I knew time would never heal.

"He was good."

I turned to see Yeshua, sitting in front of me, wearing his coarse brown robe and sandals. He quietly continued, "Crippled, but good."

"So," I cleared my throat, "if he's good, does that mean he—did he make it into, you know?"

"Heaven?"

I nodded.

"Everything is about free will," he said. "My love and free will. People only receive what they want to receive."

"Like my sister."

He nodded.

"But he never talked about you. In all our conversations, God never came up. I mean I tried, but he was pretty clear. He'd have none of it. None of . . . you."

Yeshua looked out over the water and sighed wearily. "I know."

I watched a long moment, seeing sadness fill his face. When it was clear he wouldn't answer, I finally changed subjects. "I needed you—so many times."

He turned back to me. "I know."

"And you weren't there."

"Of course, I was."

"If you were, you weren't very close."

As he often did, he cocked his head at me quizzically. "How can I get any closer than being inside you?"

Refusing to be put off, I said, "What's the point of having you inside, if I can't feel you—if I can't even hear you?"

"You did a pretty good job of hearing me in your sister's car."

"Right," I scorned. "Thanks to a dad for beating it into me."

He nodded and quietly answered, "I never play defense."

I shot him a look. He turned and gazed back out over the water.

I took a breath and blew it out in frustration. "This whole thing—I mean, what was the purpose?"

Not looking at me, he replied, "You know."

I wanted to lie, to plead ignorance, but I knew he knew. "Abide?" I ventured. "Learning to abide in you?"

"When you abide in me, what other people say and think amounts to nothing. You're no longer a slave to their opinions."

"So—I'm free of all that?"

"When you sit with me in the heavenlies, yes, always." He turned back to me and repeated, "*Always.*"

I glanced down, shaking my head. "I've made so many mistakes." When I looked back up, he was smiling. "What?" I said.

"You're a teacher. Aren't mistakes the best way to learn?"

"Then I must be a genius."

"With practice, you will be."

I frowned.

"No one overcomes the world without practice. And no one co-rules with me without training."

"You keep saying that."

"Yes, I do."

"But it's just—I'm sorry, I just don't see how that's possible."

"Impossible is my specialty."

"All I do is fail."

"A person only fails if they refuse to learn. And so far, you've been an excellent student."

"So far?" I said. "Is this going to continue?"

"Only if you want."

"If *I* want."

"It's always your choice, Will. And regardless what you choose, know we'll always love you."

I looked out over the water.

He continued, "You're free. You're no longer a slave of seeing yourself through the lens of other people. And you're free of defining yourself by what you do."

I nodded, thinking of my last conversation in the Vice Chancellor's office. "If I'm not a college professor, then what am I?"

He smiled. "You know. And if you don't, you'll soon learn."

"*If* I choose."

"Growth is always a choice, Will. It's always up to you."

I turned to him.

"So what will it be?"

I hesitated, looked back out over the water. When I turned to him, he was smiling, a sheen of moisture in his eyes. He already knew my answer.

"Okay." I began to slowly nod. "Alright. What's next?"

His smile broke into a grin. "Another adventure."

"Adventure?" I said. "To where?"

"To becoming like me."

I looked down. "That's, that's impossible."

"Ahh," he said, with that mischievous twinkle of his, "so we're back to my favorite word."

"Impossible?" I said.

He didn't answer. And when I looked to see why not, the boat was empty. I mused a moment, then looked back out over the water feeling a strange sort of excitement—and wonder.

Soli Deo gloria

Temptation
Rendezvous with GOD
Volume Two

DISCUSSION QUESTIONS

CHAPTER ONE

It breaks my heart to see the worst of Christianity paraded around as if it's normal. The misrepresentations are so great when people ask if I'm a Christian, I often ask them what they think the term means. That's one of the reasons I've written this series as well as the novel *Eli* (a retelling of the gospel as if it happened today)—to remind us who Jesus really is and what he really wishes for his followers.

And as far as committing "intellectual suicide"—there are some great books out there proving Christ and the accuracy of Scripture; some written by authors who originally set out to disprove what they considered to be myth. One of my favorite quotes is from Josephus, a well-known Jewish historian from the first century who was *not* a follower of Christ:

> *Now there was about this time Jesus, a wise man, if it be lawful to call him a man, for he was a doer of wonderful works, a teacher of such men as receive*

the truth with pleasure. He drew over to him both many of the Jews and many of the Gentiles. He was the Christ and when Pilate, at the suggestion of the principal men among us, had condemned him to the cross, those that loved him at the first did not forsake him; for he appeared to them alive again on the third day; as the divine prophets had foretold these and ten thousand other wonderful things concerning him. And the tribe of Christians so named from him are not extinct at this day.[1]

1. Forgetting how the world misrepresents Jesus and his followers, what areas about his teaching do you try to ignore or find embarrassing? Might be a good place to start up some honest dialogue with him and see what happens.

CHAPTER TWO

In college, my life was galvanized when I put these three sections of Scripture together:

And we know that in all things God works for the good of those who love him, who have been called according to his purpose. (Romans 8:28)

Consider it pure joy, my brothers and sisters, whenever you face trials of many kinds, because you know that the testing of your faith produces perseverance. Let perseverance finish its work so that you may be mature and complete, not lacking anything. (James 1:2–4)

---

1. Josephus, *Antiquities* 18.3.3, pp. 63–64.

Rejoice always, pray continually, give thanks in all circumstances; for this is God's will for you in Christ Jesus. (1 Thessalonians 5:16–18)

1. How would you approach life if you really, *really* believed these verses were true?

2. Along those lines, here are a few more verses worth contemplating:

   Do you not know that we will judge angels? (1 Corinthians 6:3)

   Now if we are children, then we are heirs—heirs of God and co-heirs with Christ, if indeed we share in his sufferings in order that we may also share in his glory. (Romans 8:17)

   "To the one who is victorious, I will give the right to sit with me on my throne, just as I was victorious and sat down with my Father on his throne." (Revelation 3:21)

CHAPTER FOUR

I was captain of my tennis team in high school for two years. One of the reasons was my grandma lived a block away. So, when the coach said, "Okay, Myers, take the team for a run through the town," we took off, disappeared around the block, and hit my grandma's for milk and homemade cookies. Everyone loved me. And how many tennis matches did we win? You guessed it: zero. For some reason we just didn't have the stamina of the other schools.

1. In what areas of your life is God taking you through a workout; moving you from the mere reading of Scripture to it becoming your flesh and blood?

2. What areas of fear prevent you from stepping onto the field and playing wholeheartedly with Jesus?

CHAPTER FIVE

What an encouragement to know Jesus was tempted as we are.

> *For we do not have a high priest who is unable to empathize with our weaknesses, but we have one who has been tempted in every way, just as we are—yet he did not sin.* (Hebrews 4:15)

1. In what ways does pre-marital sex rob us of deeper communion with our future spouse?

2. In what ways do you attempt to do hand-to-hand combat with temptation, instead of running to Christ and allowing worship to push out and replace the temptation?

CHAPTER SIX

I believe we have two walls around our heart to prevent God from ruling our lives. The first is the outer wall, full of superficial excuses to deflect him from the inner wall, the real wall, that refuses to give him complete control.

1. What are the superficial walls people use today?

2. What ones are you using?

CHAPTER SEVEN

1. To what degree should Patricia's (and James 3:1) words disqualify people caught up in sin from teaching?

2. Where do grace, forgiveness, and repentance apply?

CHAPTER NINE

1. What are practical ways you can hear God's still, small voice?

2. Regarding Yeshua's comment about letters being an inferior way to communicate. Have you found this to be true?

3. Have you had emails misunderstood?

4. Is there a difference between those letters and the letters God uses in the New Testament and Jesus's letters to the seven churches in Revelation?

CHAPTER TEN

1. What are Patricia's strengths?

2. What weaknesses do we see starting to emerge?

CHAPTER ELEVEN

I have the following verses on the wall in front of my desk.

> "For as the heavens are higher than the earth,
> So are My ways higher than your ways
> And My thoughts than your thoughts.

> For as the rain and the snow come down from
>   heaven,
> And do not return there without watering the
>   earth
> And making it produce and sprout,
> And furnishing seed to the sower and bread to the
>   eater;
> So will My word be which goes forth from My
>   mouth;
> It will not return to Me empty,
> Without accomplishing what I desire,
> And without succeeding in the matter for which
>   I sent it."
> (Isaiah 55:9–11 NASB1995)

They're on my wall for several reasons. The first is to remind me that my binary requests of yes/no, or do/don't come from my only seeing a fraction of the whole picture. The second is a reminder for me to always step back. Once I've made my petitions (and made them intensely), I need to let him take over because his answers are so much better (and deeper) than my requests. Far too often I'm looking at his hand to know the situation, instead of into his eyes to know him.

1. What percentages of your prayers are answered the way you wish?

2. How does this impact your faith?

3. Recall two or three prayer requests which were answered more deeply than you expected.

CHAPTER THIRTEEN

As the father of daughters and a past instructor for the rape and sexual abuse center of my county, the issue of sexual assault is *very* important to me, as it should be for all of us. Yet, the rush to judgment is also a concern.

1. How do we find the balance?

2. How do we apply that balance in both our thoughts and our actions?

CHAPTER FOURTEEN

1. In what ways could Will start having an impact on Patricia's relationship with God?

2. Is there a difference between seeking holiness and seeking Jesus?

3. Is there anything Will can learn from Patricia?

CHAPTER FIFTEEN

1. Is Patricia's pastor giving her the wrong advice?

2. How could it be properly applied?

3. How could it be misapplied?

CHAPTER SIXTEEN

Before writing this chapter, the Lord and I had some lengthy discussions about drawing parallels between enslavement to pornography and ultra-religion. That said:

1. Is Yeshua being unfair?

2. Where do you agree or disagree?

3. In what ways is being religious a plus?

4. How is it possible to pursue holiness while avoiding the negative aspects of religion?

CHAPTER EIGHTEEN

1. In what practical ways can you push back outside pressure through worship?

2. When are you most persuaded to believe your worship is hypocritical?

3. Experiencing God in the present instead of the past or the future takes practice. What are some practical ways to improve this?

CHAPTER TWENTY

Some of my TV news friends tell me their job is to entertain first and to inform second. After all, entertainment supposedly gets higher ratings. Their mantra? Sell the news through "Tears and Fears"—find something to make the audience tear up (a person crying on camera always helps), or find stories that create fear. These days, I would add a third— show people in conflict with one another (any writer will agree conflict makes great entertainment). So . . .

1. How can we inoculate ourselves from news as "entertainment" and still remain informed citizens?

CHAPTER TWENTY-ONE

Instead of seeing himself as God sees him (where he is loved the same on his worst days as on his best), Will sees himself through the lens of people's opinion. So many of his choices reveal this—from his love for classical writers who speak to him but don't see him (or judge him), to his solitude on the island (no people equals no judgment), even to his failed marriage. And now, if he chooses, he can be free. Below are three "false lenses" Henri Nouwen believes people see themselves through. We spoke of this in the Discussion Questions of *Volume One*, but it's worth repeating. They are:

- People's opinions of you
- Your accomplishments
- What you have

1. Which of the three most seriously impact you?

2. If you agree to his help how might God free you of them?

CHAPTER TWENTY-THREE

Will has entered the crucible. But it's still his choice whether to be free or remain enslaved.

1. Is there an area in your life where you're struggling to say yes to God?

2. What comfort can you take in knowing Jesus went through similar struggles of human will versus God's will?

CHAPTER TWENTY-FIVE

C. S. Lewis used the term *severe mercy*.

1. How does this term apply to Will's life?

2. How is God's severe mercy currently playing out in yours?

CHAPTER TWENTY-SEVEN

Over and over again, Yeshua insists God never plays defense—he is an economical God who will use everything, if we let him. Which brings us back to Romans 8:28, James 1:2–4, and 1 Thessalonians 5:16–18; particularly how God used Will's painful summer with his father so many decades earlier to help save his niece and her baby.

1. What dark areas in your life have you seen God use for good?

2. What areas are you still waiting to see?

Finally, Will frequently picks on himself and the opposite sex for being so different from one another. And yet, his "manly skills" of working with metal and repairing cars works in perfect harmony with the more tender and experienced "women's skills" when they're involved in delivering the baby.

3. How often do we try forcing ourselves to be alike, when the very diversity between men and women often makes us more complete?

A sample from the next installment:

COMMUNE

Rendezvous with GOD
Volume Three

BY THE TIME I returned, Dr. Martin was already seated with Amber and Darlene in the waiting room. When they looked up, I knew the news was bad.

"What's wrong?" I said. "How's the baby; is she okay?"

Martin rose to his feet and motioned to the empty chair. "Please, sit."

"What happened? What went wrong?"

"Nothing went wrong. The procedure went perfectly as planned."

"Then—"

"I'm afraid Billie-Jean's condition is worse than we expected."

The room shifted and I adjusted to keep my balance.

He motioned back to the chair. "Please."

I shook my head.

He continued. "The catherization went as planned but once we reached her heart—"

I interrupted. "Tetralogy of Fallot; you said it was Tetralogy of Fallot."

"Yes. But of a severity . . . well to be quite frank, I've never seen it to this extent."

A faint sob escaped from Amber, barely discernable, but enough for Darlene to wrap an arm around her.

Martin began a detailed explanation, but I was straining too hard to read his tone and expressions to fully grasp what he said—until I heard: "You hadn't noticed her becoming more lethargic? Irritable? Breathing more rapidly than normal?"

My anger flared, "She's our first baby, how are we supposed to know what's normal?"

Another sob from Amber, and Darlene pulled her into her arms.

I continued, "You're the one who made us wait, then turned around and postponed things even longer."

"Yes," he cleared his throat, "we had an emergency."

"And this isn't?"

"It's not necessarily—"

"So, what are you going to do? Can you fix it?"

He paused, waiting for me to take it down a notch. But I stood, glowering.

"Yes," he said. "To answer your question, it's most definitely treatable. But I suggest we operate as soon as possible."

"Operate?" The word slammed into my chest. Yes, I knew it was a possibility. But three weeks. Three weeks we'd been praying for a miracle and this is what we get? "When?" I demanded. "What does that mean?"

"I'll clear my schedule and—"

"What does that mean?"

"We'll see how she responds to this afternoon's sedative and if there are no ill effect—"

"What does that—"

He cleared his throat. "Tomorrow morning. I'd like to schedule her first thing in the morning."

He went on to rattle off the procedure, retreating to it like a wall of defense. But I barely heard. The room shifted again. Then again. Lack of food from the fasting? Who knows. Whatever the reason, the empty chair now looked more inviting.

But I refused. Somebody had to take charge. And since it wasn't going to be God . . .

I turned to the doctor. "When will you know?"

"Know?"

"About the sedative. When will you know if she's strong enough?"

"Two hours, maybe three. I suggest you grab a bite to eat and—"

"I'm staying here," Amber said, her voice muffled inside Darlene's embrace.

"It may be longer depending upon—"

"I'm staying here."

He turned to me and I nodded. "She stays." Then I added, "Can she go back there and sit with her?"

He hesitated.

"It's a simple question, Doctor. Can she sit with her baby while she recovers?"

"Yes."

Amber pulled from Darlene and wiped her face.

"There's one more thing," he said.

I looked at him; my patience gone.

"If she's ready," he cleared his throat. "If she's ready, I'd like to admit Billie-Jean to the hospital tonight."

"What?"

"To keep an eye on her. This will give us plenty of time to properly prep her before surgery."

"Tonight?"

"A precaution. To continue surveillance and to prepare her."

I felt all eyes turn to me, waiting for a decision. I hesitated, weighed the consequences, then gave my answer. "Yes."

Previous Praise for Bill Myers's Novels

Blood of Heaven

"With the chill of a Robin Cooke techno-thriller and the spiritual depth of a C. S. Lewis allegory, this book is a fast-paced, action-packed thriller." —Angela Hunt, *NY Times* best-selling author

"Enjoyable and provocative. I wish I'd thought of it!" —Frank E. Peretti, *This Present Darkness*

ELI

"The always surprising Myers has written another clever and provocative tale." —Booklist

"With this thrilling and ominous tale, Myers continues to shine brightly in speculative fiction based upon biblical truth. Highly recommended." —*Library Journal*

"Myers weaves a deft, affecting tale." —*Publishers Weekly* **The Face of God**

"Strong writing, edgy . . . replete with action . . ." —*Publishers Weekly*

Fire of Heaven

"I couldn't put the *Fire of Heaven* down. Bill Myers's writing is crisp, fast-paced, provocative . . . A very compelling story."
—Francine Rivers, *NY Times* best-selling author

Soul Tracker

"Soul Tracker provides a treat for previous fans of the author but also a fitting introduction to those unfamiliar with his work. I'd recommend the book to anyone, initiated or not. But be careful to check your expectations at the door . . . it's not what you think it is." —Brian Reaves, *Fuse* magazine

"Thought provoking and touching, this imaginative tale blends elements of science fiction with Christian theology."
—*Library Journal*

"Myers strikes deep into the heart of eternal truth with this imaginative first book of the Soul Tracker series. Readers will be eager for more." —*Romantic Times* magazine

Angel of Wrath

"Bill Myers is a genius." —Lee Stanley, producer, Gridiron Gang

Saving Alpha

"When one of the most creative minds I know gets the best idea he's ever had and turns it into a novel, it's fasten-your-seat-belt time. This one will be talked about for a long time."
—Jerry B. Jenkins, author of *Left Behind*

"An original masterpiece." —Dr. Kevin Leman, best-selling author

"If you enjoy white-knuckle, page-turning suspense, with a brilliant blend of cutting-edge apologetics, *Saving Alpha* will grab you for a long, long time." —Beverly Lewis, *NY Times* best-selling author

"I've never seen a more powerful and timely illustration of the incarnation. Bill Myers has a way of making the gospel accessible and relevant to readers of all ages. I highly recommend this book." —Terri Blackstock, *NY Times* best-selling author

"A brilliant novel that feeds the mind and heart, *Saving Alpha* belongs at the top of your reading list." —Angela Hunt, *NY Times* best-selling author

"*Saving Alpha* is a rare combination that is both entertaining and spiritually provocative. It has a message of deep spiritual significance that is highly relevant for these times." —Paul Cedar, Chairman, Mission America Coalition

"Once again Myers takes us into imaginative and intriguing depths, making us feel, think and ponder all at the same time. Relevant and entertaining. *Saving Alpha* is not to be missed." —James Scott Bell, best-selling author

The Voice

"A crisp, express-train read featuring 3D characters, cinematic settings and action, and, as usual, a premise I wish I'd thought of. Succeeds splendidly! Two thumbs up!" —Frank E. Peretti, *This Present Darkness*

"Nonstop action and a brilliantly crafted young heroine will keep readers engaged as this adventure spins to its thought-provoking conclusion. This book explores the intriguing concept of God's power as not only the creator of the universe, but as its very essence." —Kris Wilson, *CBA* magazine

"It's a real 'what if ?' book with plenty of thrills . . . that will definitely create questions all the way to its thought-provoking finale. The success of Myers's stories is a sweet combination of a believable storyline, intense action, and brilliantly crafted, yet flawed characters." —Dale Lewis, TitleTrakk.com

The Seeing

"Compels the reader to burn through the pages. Cliff-hangers abound, and the stakes are raised higher and higher as the story progresses—intense, action-shocking twists!" —Title Trakk.com

When the Last Leaf Falls

"A wonderful novella . . . Any parent will warm to the humorous reminiscences and the loving exasperation of this father for his strong-willed daughter . . . Compelling characters and fresh, vibrant anecdotes of one family's faith journey." —*Publishers Weekly*